NAPLES, OR DIE!

1943. The British 8th Army had crossed over from Messina to Reggio and 'Scoop' Britwell, a fighting war correspondent, suffered from battle fatigue. Always on the lookout for his brother, Captain 'Tufty' Britwell of the Home Counties Commandos, he's captured by the Germans where he befriends Lieutenant Rawson, an L.C.T. skipper, and Dusty Lewis, a Pioneer. When he is released by British troops, 'Scoop' finally catches up with 'Tufty' and together they face the fighting in Naples . . .

DAVID BINGLEY

◆

NAPLES, OR DIE!

Complete and Unabridged

LINFORD
Leicester

First published in Great Britain

First Linford Edition
published 2009

British Library CIP Data

Bingley, David, *1920 –*
   Naples, or die! - - (Linford mystery library)
   1. Great Britain. Army. Army, Eighth.- -Fiction.
   2. World War, *1939 – 1945*- -Campaigns- -Italy
   - -Fiction. 3. Prisoners of war- -Fiction.
   4. Detective and mystery stories.
   5. Large type books.
   I. Title II. Series III. Chesham, Henry, *1920 –*
   823.9′14–dc22

ISBN 978–1–84782–750–0

Published by
F. A. Thorpe (Publishing)
Anstey, Leicestershire

Set by Words & Graphics Ltd.
Anstey, Leicestershire
Printed and bound in Great Britain by
T. J. International Ltd., Padstow, Cornwall

1

Half-way up a rock-strewn hillside over-looking the wartime Sicilian port of Messina, a solitary Englishman flinched as shells from six hundred artillery weapons hissed and whined through the cloudless sky above him on their way to a scattered burial in mangled heaps of earth, stone and twisted metal on Italian soil.

Harry Britwell, now a war correspondent, and formerly a crime reporter on the London Daily Globe, was far from comfortable in the broiling sun. His tongue frequently explored his thin dry lips.

Britwell was tall and sinewy, long of limb and surprisingly fit for a man of thirty-five. Two years in the sunny Mediterranean had bleached his fair hair to the colour of straw, and his skin was almost as dark as that of the native Sicilians.

His binoculars were trained on the narrow Straits of Messina, where many squat landing craft were slowly crossing to the mainland of Italy, wallowing in each other's wakes. Normally, he would have enthused over the sight, but after witnessing the conquest of Sicily in thirty-eight rigorous days, he was suffering from a tiredness akin to battle-fatigue.

Even as he watched, however, he was making up his mind to move on, to further his reputation for always being up with the action, whether on land or sea. After fitting a pair of green-tinted sun glasses over his eyes he set off down the slope towards the shell-torn harbour which was alive with khaki-clad ants.

His war correspondent's pass took him into the harbour right behind a naval jeep which drew up before the office of the British Naval-Officer-in-Charge. A stiff-backed lieutenant-commander with a familiar face climbed out of the vehicle. He had saluted the sentry and was about to enter the office when Britwell caught up with him.

'Pardon me, sir, aren't you Lieutenant-Commander Newbold?'

Newbold had a pronounced Roman nose and a thin hard mouth. Close to, he looked his thirty-eight years, but some of the stiffness went out of him as he recognised the newcomer. His small mouth broadened into a passable smile.

'Why, yes, I'm Newbold. And you're Britwell, the war correspondent! Haven't seen you since Narvik!'

They shook hands warmly and stepped round the side of the building. Britwell removed his sun glasses, and the two of them looked deep into each other's eyes, sharing mutual respect which dated from the Norwegian naval action.

Newbold went on: 'I've heard a buzz that you nearly bought it on a Malta convoy run last year. Was there any truth in it?'

Britwell fingered two thin lines of scar tissue, one on each cheek from his upper lip to near his ears, under the cheekbones. They resembled cats' whiskers drawn with actors' makeup wax.

He said: 'Not really. A large piece of

shrapnel burst on the Air Defence platform of a battlewagon during Operation Pedestal and gashed my face. I got off lightly, though. The Midshipman up there lost a lump of flesh out of his forearm.'

Newbold smiled again. 'I guessed as much. You'd better be careful when you get back to Soho, the villains will think you've been chivved!'

Britwell laughed heartily for the first time in several days. He was about to utter a droll remark when a voice carried to them through the shuttered windows of the office behind them.

'Any sign of Lieutenant-Commander Newbold yet?'

The reply, in a much humbler voice, was too quiet to be heard out of doors. Newbold sniffed. 'That's the Commodore asking for me. I'll have to get in there in a moment. It's grand to have met you again. Is there anything I can do before I shove off?'

'Yes, get me across to Reggio by the next boat.'

Newbold thought rapidly. 'Look here,

you'll never get across with the second wave, but you might do it with the third, in about an hour. Look out for L.C.T. 17. She'll be tying up at the North Mole as soon as she gets in. The skipper's a friend of mine. Lofty Rawson. He was with me in the Tobruk do. Tell him I sent you along, but don't let any of the other passengers hear you. Lofty will take you, even if he has to hide you in his own bunk.'

Britwell thanked him profusely and moved away. It was moments like this, he reflected, which made his own brand of self-imposed frontline reporting worth while. Old Newbold was a typical product of Dartmouth Naval College; steeped in the old idea of naval discipline as practised in the R.N., but an out-and-out sailor to his backbone.

In that Narvik fjord the destroyer's bows had been blown off and the Captain killed. It had been Newbold's hour of triumph when as a somewhat inexperienced first lieutenant he had been thrust into command. The epic way in which he had brought home half a ship had gone down in the annals of naval history at the

Admiralty. It had also figured promi-
nently in Britwell's despatch from the
front.

In spite of the screaming shells
overhead, and the perpetual tramp of
soldiers' feet going to their points of
embarkation, loneliness crowded in upon
Britwell as he strolled towards the North
Mole.

As he approached each waiting Army
unit, he glanced eagerly at their shoulder
flashes, but he was disappointed every
time. He was looking for signs of the 3rd
Home Counties Commando, the outfit in
which his younger brother, Jack, was
serving as a captain.

Jack was his only surviving relative. By
the law of averages, he figured, the two of
them were bound to run across each
other some time or another. Provided that
the chance did not come too late.

★ ★ ★

Lieutenant Colin Rawson, skipper of the
landing craft L.C.T. 17, was a confirmed
optimist.

At the time when Britwell was conferring with Newbold, the battered landing craft was jockeying its way back to port after surviving a hammering in the first assault.

Rawson yawned. He rested his bulk on the squat bridge rail, right aft, and called down to the wheelhouse, which was situated below and forward of him, immediately above the well deck where tanks and men taking passage were normally housed.

'Well, we came through that little schemozzle all right, Swain!' he called to the cox'n.

Petty Officer Jones, a brown-eyed red-headed Welshman from Cardiff, glanced back at his skipper, his face still flushed with the recent excitement.

'I never expected we'd have much trouble, sir. Got a fine row of tracer holes here, across the front of the wheelhouse to show for it, though.'

'Pity about the Carley float, too,' Rawson went on. 'We might need that some day!'

He was referring to the loss of a raft,

the moorings of which had been sheered off by the sudden burst of 88mm. shells, near the beach. The float had flopped gracefully overboard and wallowed off at a time when they were too hard pressed to do anything about it.

'I wouldn't worry, sir. It's better than the bridge going over the side, you'll allow!'

Rawson emitted a deep belly laugh. A pimply-faced young able-seaman who was sharing the bridge with him as lookout and messenger, joined in the merriment. The skipper was his favourite of bar-room conversation. The seaman studied him afresh, although he knew his C.O. better than his own father, who had been away in the Far East for a couple of years.

He saw Rawson as a big, jovial mountain of flesh and muscle, six-feet two-inches in height and weighing at least fifteen stones. A tufty, sprouting brown beard made his round face look even fatter, and a thinning patch under the battered peaked-cap furthered his like-ness to a light-hearted monk.

Rawson's discipline, to say the least, was unusual. Even Captain's Defaulters had been known at times to appear more like a variety turn when the skipper had been on form.

The skipper groaned as the harbour entrance loomed towards them. He pushed the engine-room telegraph to 'Half Ahead' and called: 'Starboard fifteen, Swain!'

Slowly, the unwieldy, blunt-bowed craft answered.

With a rare flash of insight, the seaman reflected that a good L.C.T. skipper could not really get on without a fine sense of humour. The job was too frustrating.

Ten minutes later, they approached the North Mole.

★ ★ ★

Waiting on the Mole for the L.C.T. were twenty perspiring, apprehensive Sappers, in the charge of two N.C.O.s and a silent aloof captain. As the ship tied up, the captain ordered his men to their feet. He was a small dapper man named Carter; a native of Birmingham, with a bristling moustache. Grey hair showed at his temples under the tin hat. He watched Rawson clump across to the port side of the bridge and shout into the superstructure.

'What about a wet all round, Scotty?'

A seaman in a soiled apron, overalls and a grubby white cap cover, stepped onto the quarterdeck and squinted up at the bridge. 'Water's nearly boiling, Skip. Be about ten minutes.'

Rawson nodded. He scratched his beard, which was irritable with dried perspiration and salt spray. Further forward, on the port side, Petty Officer Jones was supervising the rigging of a gangway. Beyond it, on the Mole, Captain Carter fidgeted from one foot to the other. Rawson filled his chest and shouted across the intervening space, above the noise of the bombardment.

'You making the next trip with us, sir?'

Carter blinked, did a nervous salute which Rawson ignored and finally nodded.

'Right, you can get your men aboard any time you like. Plenty of room for 'em in the stowage space!'

Carter acknowledged, and Rawson thumped back to the voice-pipes in size ten seaboots. He blew down the engine-room pipe, cleared his throat, and said: 'That you, Jock?'

A weary voice replied: 'Who else would want to be down in this sweat chamber, if not me?'

Rawson grinned. He ignored the rudeness and went on: 'Come up and have a word with me as soon as you can manage it. And by the way, there's a wet of tea just brewing.'

Still grinning, he moved easily down the port bridge ladder and disappeared into the superstructure, ducking his head carefully as he went through the door.

$\star$ $\star$ $\star$

'Thank Gawd that infernal bombardment's stopped! We've either run out of ammo, or else some bright basket has finally got round to the idea it's wasteful!'

Ten minutes had gone by, and the speaker on the Mole was a short, alert individual with a bruised and flattened lower lip. Corporal 'Nipper' Harris was a native of Bow. Some ten years earlier he had been a promising flyweight boxer.

The man to whom he addressed the remarks wore the same Pioneer Corps flashes. His head also bore the marks of the pugilist's trade, but Dusty Lewis would have made three of Nipper Harris. He was a former southern-area heavy-weight boxing champion. Punishment had taken a greater toll of him than it had of his friend. He had a cauliflower ear, a broken nose and a deep-set slitted eyes, due to many cuts in that region.

Lewis ignored Harris's remarks. He said: 'Cor, what wouldn't I give to be the driver of that machine!'

Harris peered up at the mobile crane, operating just behind them. Hanging from the hook was a shining, yellow-painted bulldozer, on its way into the craft's hold.

'Come off it, cocker. You know you'd be a bloody menace in charge of that thing!' Harris replied, uncharitably.

Lewis grunted and became silent.

Instead, he watched closely as the 'dozer was manoeuvred over the vessel's well deck and slowly lowered into place, controlled by signals from the cox'n.

'All right to go aboard now, Corp?'

The speaker was one of ten other Pioneers who had been loaned to the Royal Engineers for general duties on the beaches of Reggio. Harris squinted across to the ship's quarterdeck. Captain Carter was intent on activities the other side of the harbour. The little corporal grunted.

He said: 'Yer, I expect so, mate. Get your kit on board. We'll be with you in a minute.'

Soon the bulldozer had disappeared from sight, and the Mole was clear, except for the two ex-boxers and the crane driver.

'Not much of a packet, is she?' Harris commented dismally.

Lewis turned slowly and took in the ship's features. The light grey Mediterranean paint looked as if it hadn't had a fresh coat since World War I. It was grimy and peeling. The guardrail was dented in several places where the vessel had been in collision with jetties and other craft of a similar type which were difficult to manoeuvre.

'Aw, I expect she'll get us there all right,' Lewis answered, after a pause. He started to walk towards the gangway. 'You comin' then, Nip?'

The big man was still thinking how good it would feel to be a bulldozer driver instead of humping and digging all the time like a pack animal. Harris followed him reluctantly. He did not like the sea. Even a joyride from Southend pier was enough to upset his queasy stomach. He wondered if anyone else would be seasick.

★ ★ ★

Harry Britwell dashed along the jetty just as Petty Offcer Jones was taking in the gangway.

'Just a minute, P.O.!' he called breathlessly. 'You'll have room for one more, I should think!'

Jones straightened up. He made a gesture for the seamen to hold on a moment, and regarded the newcomer with ill-concealed suspicion. He glanced at the bronzed man's shoulder flashes. A blasted reporter! A civvy masquerading in khaki. If there was anyone Jones hated, it was a non-combatant. And this one looked a right Charlie.

With his fists on his hips and his head thrust forward belligerently, he replied in his best lower deck manner: 'We got no instructions about newspaper correspondents, mate. We're just about to push off with a full load. Better step back if you don't want your bats crushed.'

The five seamen of the working party exchanged grins. None of them could bear Jones needling them, but when he was having a go at a civvy that was different. They wanted the civvy to protest, so that the cox'n would come out with a real torrent of abuse; something to make the pongos' hair curl.

Britwell grinned cynically. 'I've got a message from the N.O.I.C.'s office. Better tell the skipper before you push off!'

Jones knew he would have to do something about that. He glared round the side-and-cable party, daring them to show any interest.

'All right, then. I'll get the skipper,' he conceded. 'But you'd better stay where you are till you get the okay to come aboard!'

'Very well, Mister Petty Officer, sir!' Britwell gave the cox'n a mock naval salute. The N.C.O.'s neck reddened as he stamped away to the quarterdeck and disappeared through the wide door.

He found Rawson standing by a hatch with the P.O. Motor Mechanic, who was saying: 'Well, all right, Skipper. Don't forget I've warned you the port engine might pack up if it overheats again. That's all. The responsibility's yours.'

Rawson beamed down at him. 'The responsibility has always been mine, Jock. Now you've made your report, get back to your Turkish Bath and see it damned well doesn't pack up! It may come as news to you, but we've got a war going on up top here!'

The disgruntled Scot went off down his ladder, muttering profanities and screwing a piece of cotton waste as though he was strangling somebody. Rawson shrugged his beefy shoulders, fumbled for a cigarette, and turned to Jones.

'Well, what's the buzz now then, Swain?' he asked, talking round the fag as he lit it. 'Company want deck chairs, or what?'

Jones grimaced. 'There's a long lanky newspaper bloke on the jetty. Tried to get himself aboard just now, cocky as you like. When I stopped him, he said he had a message from the N.O.I.C.'s office. Do you want to see him?'

Rawson blew out a cloud of smoke. He grinned, knowing how Jones felt about such people. 'I'd better take a look at him, hadn't I? After all, he might be speaking the truth. And you never know, sailing orders might have been cancelled. They may be sending us straight home for a long leave!'

In spite of his ill-humour, Jones grinned. 'Not much fear of that, sir. Might get survivors' leave very shortly, though.'

Rawson peered through the open door. His eyesight was very keen. From where he was, he could distinguish the scar tissue on Britwell's face. He whistled, and Jones stepped up behind him to take another look.

'Oh, come off it, Taff, boy,' Rawson remonstrated. 'Give credit where it's due. That's no ordinary reporter. It's the boy himself. Scoop Britwell — Our Man at the Front. He nearly bought it on two or three occasions through being in the thick of the action.'

Rawson rolled the cigarette around his mouth with his tongue.

Jones swallowed hard. The rancour was leaving him now. He began to feel a little ashamed of himself.

'Know what they say about him in Gib and Malta, Swain?' Rawson went on. 'They say when his time comes, he'll probably have his head blown off through standing in front of a Jerry gun.'

The two of them emerged into the bright sunlight, and Rawson waved Britwell aboard. Their handshake on the tiny quarterdeck was witnessed by many curious eyes. Britwell explained what he wanted and mentioned Newbold.

'Say no more, chum. I know Newbold, and I've heard of you. You're very welcome. Come on the bridge if you like. We're just about to slip. I'll be glad of a chin-wag once I've got this perishing barge out into the Straits.'

Britwell eagerly accepted the offer.

2

Through Rawson's binoculars, the beaches at Reggio presented quite a spectacle.

Four huge American tank landing ships lay nose in to the shingle with bow doors agape. Smaller assault craft were moored alongside of them, being loaded with stores and ammunition. As the smaller craft plied their way back and forth, war materials were piling up on the beach with alarming rapidity.

At that distance everything looked mildly chaotic. The tiny figures of Pioneer Corps men scrambled and scampered, lugging ammo boxes and the like, trying to keep pace with the build up. Off to the right, a long line of tanks was threading its way slowly forward towards a line of shabby trees to the rear of the beach.

Further up the toe, he could see the bulk of Liberty ships and large numbers of small warships of all types. A large, white-painted hospital ship stood out from the rest with a gigantic red cross painted across an awning right aft.

Everything was much the same in appearance as when they had been over the previous time, Rawson decided. Only there were more men and materials ashore, of course.

A mile or so inland, German 88mm. guns were keeping up a steady fusillade against the beaches and the men who sought doggedly to encroach inland. Already the Italians who had manned the forty-odd guns which were supposed to command the Straits had given in. A bombardment by the sixteen-inch battle-ships, *Nelson* and *Rodney* — ably backed up by smaller warships — had hastened their surrender.

The British had expected this, remembering how the Italians had given in by the thousand in North Africa, and then again in Sicily. If they had known how few Allied troops were engaged in the assault on Calabria, perhaps they would have remained brave for a little longer. In all, the Allies were using only two divisions.

The beaches themselves, and the hills

immediately to the rear, were constantly criss-crossed by streams of bright tracer going both ways. To Rawson it seemed scarcely possible that units frantically working on the beach could possibly stay alive under it. Every now and then, a great cloud of smoke and debris went up, tinged with orange flame, as some unfortunate Briton went too close to a concealed mine.

Suddenly a formation of Stukas whipped across the sky from the north-east, heading for the beached vessels with only one purpose in view. Bombs, like tiny silver pellets dropped from them, hurtling towards the concourse of shipping on the north side.

With equal suddenness, a flak-ship — out of sight behind the hospital ship — let go with all its armaments at the raiders. One of the first three developed a smoke trail almost at once, and the second group of three turned sharply to port, heading for the beaches. As though synchronised by a single director, all the small guns of the landings ships opened up on them. The planes came on steadily, and in a matter of seconds the sky was grey with small shell bursts.

Falling bombs raised great gouts of water around the ships offshore, and one assault craft lurched skyward to fall back under the sea in its last plunge.

'Stuka bomber 'eadin' this way, sir!' the port lookout bellowed, in a raucous Yorkshire accent.

Rawson whipped the glasses from his eyes and blinked upwards. The plane was coming straight at them in a long whistling dive. Right aft on the vessel's quarters, the L.C.'s gunners were standing behind their two-pounder pom-poms, waiting for the right moment to open up.

The skipper turned to them. 'Don't waste your ammo, lads!' he shouted. 'She's had it anyway!'

Seconds later, the burning plane's machine-guns opened up, ripping into the fore part of the superstructure and clanging on the port side.

'All personnel take cover!' Rawson yelled again.

He thought: I hope to God they don't

pierce the petrol tanks. We'd go up like Vesuvius!

Lower than mast height, the Stuka roared over them. Britwell, hazarding a quick glance upwards, saw the strained face of the pilot set in desperation as he worked his guns for the last time. For maybe two or three seconds after he had passed over, the crew's heads stayed down . . . then, just as he struck the sea's unyielding surface with a mighty splash, the heads bobbed up in time to witness his end.

The wings came away. The tail folded, and the fuselage telescoped like a flattened can. There was no sign of life in the shattered mass of metal as it sank slowly amid a thousand bursting air bubbles.

Excited cries broke from the passengers in the well-deck, too low to see what had happened. 'Stone the crows,' a wag was exclaiming, 'I thought for a moment this old barge was goin' to be me coffin — a metal one!'

The laughs which followed this sally were dry and off-key. It was a laughter born of relief rather than humour. Rawson accepted one of Britwell's duty-frees. He was lighting it when Jones called up from the wheelhouse.

'How about it, Skipper? The beach is pretty congested right ahead. Do I take her south or north?'

Rawson waved his hand to show he had heard. He studied the beach situation again through the binoculars, all the while puffing furiously at his cigarette. Britwell was thinking this was going to be some trip. He sniffed keenly at the air about him. For most of the trip he had felt drowsy with the tang of salt and seaweed, but now the acrid smells of smoke and cordite were cloying with it.

Rawson came to a decision. 'We'll take her south, I think, Swain. Aim to put her in about half a cable's length away from the southernmost landing ship.'

'Aye, aye, sir.' Jones swung his wheel over to starboard. Rawson adjusted the engine-room telegraph. Beneath them, the revs dropped as the speed was cut by half. Rawson smiled as the revs died. All the way over he had been expecting the port engine to pack up, but by luck — and the skill of the engineer — it had kept going.

If it packed up on the way back, it would not be so serious. He leaned over the bridge rail and called down to Captain Carter who had gone into the well-deck to make the crossing the hard way with his men.

'Better have your men stand-to, Captain!' he warned.

Carter came to his feet with alacrity. He ran a spatulate finger and thumb across his bristly moustache — a nervous gesture of which he was totally unaware. 'Very well, Skipper,' he called back. 'We'll be ready!'

Minutes later, the blunt bows grated on shingle and the ship shuddered to a halt. The bow door dropped open with a great creek and a resounding splash.

'All right, passengers,' Rawson roared, 'it's all yours! Don't scoff too much fruit on the way!'

★ ★ ★

Britwell thanked Rawson profusely for the trip over. He shook hands and waded ashore, his agile brain soaking up impressions as he went. He had to leap for his life as the bulldozer hurtled through the shallow water, scattering sizeable waves to right and left from its flailing caterpillars. He watched it as it surged ashore, the great rammer held high. The driver, a grinning sapper, gave him the thumbs-up sign, but it passed unnoticed.

On the beach itself, the shingle and sand had already been carved into deep ruts by wheels and caterpillars. A long line of Canadians were wading ashore to his left from the nearest landing ship. He could not fail to admire their nonchalant expressions as their feet slithered and slipped in the shallow water. They were taking it like excited schoolboys having a paddle.

Back up the beach, a tall naval officer in khaki tropical rig was calling out movement orders over a loud hailer.

Britwell dodged through the great heaps of material, and the sweating working parties which were humping it further inland. He gravitated towards the beach control officer, not yet quite sure of where he wanted to go.

The officer blinked when he saw the war correspondent. His prominent Adam's apple rippled in his throat. His silent lips mouthed 'War Correspondent' and his stiff, dark brows slid up his forehead.

'Better watch how you tread up the beach,' he said curtly, 'there's still a lot of it not cleared by the Engineers.'

Britwell thanked him and moved further to his right, into the tracks of the tanks which had recently disappeared from view. Sharp bursts of automatic fire were being exchanged every few seconds between the buildings on the outskirts of the town, not many yards beyond the drooping line of trees. He halted at the trees, deciding prudently that he had advanced far enough. He sat himself down at the base of one of the trees and took a swig from his water bottle.

From this vantage point he could see much of what was going on. With another of his duty-free cigarettes stuck at a sharp angle in the corner of his mouth, he began to mentally write the scene before him.

⋆   ⋆   ⋆

Quite near the place where they had stepped ashore, the Royal Engineers and Pioneers had blended in with others of their respective units. There were two bulldozers at work, manned by sappers who were closely watched by Captain Carter.

The officer who had been in charge before Carter's arrival had promptly disappeared somewhere for a smoke.

Dusty Lewis had set to work with a will, doing twice as much fetching and carrying of ammunition boxes as any other man present. With his shirt stripped off, he displayed a magnificent set of shoulder and chest muscles which rippled and twitched as he flexed them. Nipper Harris tagged along behind him, angered at having to hump boxes in spite of his N.C.O.'s stripes.

He read again the message on the heart tattooed across his mighty friend's left

29

bicep. It said, *Leonard loves Lucy*. Harris muttered to himself. He said inaudibly: 'Gawd 'elp Lucy. It's a wonder 'e 'asn't been 'ad up for crushin' 'er to death!'

The two teams of Pioneers were stacking the ammunition boxes on large trolleys which were to be pulled away up the beach by the 'dozers. All went well for a half-hour. Then, without any warning, the bulldozer belonging to the other team touched off a mine buried in the sand.

Everyone stopped what they were doing and stared towards it. The explosive had been detonated under one of the tracks, which was unfortunate. When the flying sand and pebbles subsided and the smoke cleared, it was seen that the machine was wrecked. Furthermore, the driver was in need of immediate attention. He lay slumped across his seat, bleeding from several cuts and gashes occasioned by flying metal splinters.

The other team of Pioneers were quickly moved across to join the second group. Soon the trolley behind their 'dozer was loaded to capacity. The sapper started his machine and bumped away towards the trees.

The Pioneers straightened their backs and allowed themselves to go limp. Carter hesitated for a moment, then said: 'You Pioneers, take a crate apiece and follow the machine up the beach. We've no time for rests. There could be an air-raid at any moment!'

Some of the tired, sweat-streaked faces looked mutinous, but Lewis immediately hefted a couple of boxes onto his right shoulder and paced off after the machine. Others glared after him, but he was not the sort of chap to risk calling a blackleg. They picked up one box apiece and followed him, dropping further behind at every step.

The second bulldozer started to go temperamental. It coughed to a bumpy halt. Lewis caught up with it. He hoisted his boxes onto the packed trailer, moved round it and pulled up the bonnet. The driver waited, chewing at his nails and peering back at Captain Carter. Lewis' bloodshot eyes gleamed as he tinkered with the plugs, and tapped the carburettor.

The irate Engineer officer was no more than three yards away from them when the driver started her up again. Reluctantly, she coughed herself back to life. Lewis stepped back, rubbing his broken nose. He beamed as she moved past him.

All went well for a while. But it seemed as if there was a jinx on the machines. Two trips later, a clutch shot out. The driver gave an anguished cry and hugged his wrist. It was badly dislocated. He would do no more driving this invasion.

Lewis hauled him out of the seat as if he weighed no more than a baby. In a flash he was behind the controls. It would take an extraordinary clutch to throw *his* wrist out. He set the machine in motion, thrilling at the power under him. He coaxed it, and it took him up the beach without trouble. At the dumping spot, he unhitched the trailer.

Minutes later, he was back by the waves, grinning all over his scar-pitted face. Half a dozen men passed him, going up the beach to unload the trolley he had delivered. He never saw them. Carter stared at him, wondering at this new development. He decided he ought to assert himself.

He called: 'Hey, you there, in the bulldozer! That's not a job for a Pioneer. Better turn it over to one of the sappers!'

He looked round the Royal Engineers near him. None of them met his eyes. Nobody wanted the job of driving the temperamental machine which had thrown their mate's wrist out. Carter hesitated. He glanced back at Lewis. The big man had either not heard him, or decided to ignore him.

Carter hesitated again. Nipper Harris quickly connected up the second trailer. Lewis called back over his shoulder.

'All ready there, Nip?'

'Ready when you are, mate!'

Apparently the corporal had not heard Carter, either. The officer rubbed at his moustache, torn with indecision. When the noisy diesel-engine started up again, he decided not to bother enforcing his command. Nobody seemed to care.

Lewis roared off up the beach, humming 'Roll out the barrel' rather tunelessly. He was like a kid with a new toy.

By late tea, order prevailed on the beach.

In the middle of the afternoon, a low-flying Messerschmitt had shot up a small heap of ammo cases, causing five casualties, but the incident had been quickly forgotten.

Strangely enough, Rawson's L.C.T. was still where it had landed. When they wanted to get under way again, the port engine had not responded. Rawson had wisely taken time out to give his engineers a fair crack at her. It had taken a couple of hours for the shaft to cool. By the time Jock said it was safe to start her up again, the tide had receded and try as they might with both engines working hard in reverse the obstinate craft would not slide off the pebbles into deeper water.

Nipper Harris watched Carter move off up the beach to check the materials at the other end. As soon as he felt he was unobserved, he slipped down to the water's edge.

He nudged Petty Officer Jones, who was standing there, hands on hips, frowning up at the closed bow doors. The cox'n was in a niggly mood. He wrinkled his freckled forehead, and peered down at Harris.

'Hello, there, Shorty,' he said, 'what now then? You been an' conquered Italy in half a day, or what?'

'Not so much o' the smart talk, Cox'n. I came down 'ere to do you a favour. You're stuck, aren't you? Till next high tide by the looks o' things. Now if you was to slip me a packet o' fags, quietly like, I could tell yer a way to 'ave the old barge in deep water in, say — ten minutes. Now, what do yer say?'

Jones laughed without humour. 'Come off it, Shorty. What have you in mind? Going to ask your big friend to push us off single-handed — like flaming Atlas or somebody? No, I don't go for anything like that. Besides, I haven't got any fags on me, in any case.'

But Harris persisted. 'You do want to get back to Messina, don't yer? It ain't much of a place, but it's better than this ruddy beach by a long chalk. Take a chance, won't yer? I'll trust yer, an' the skipper'll think you're a ruddy wizard.

You can pass it off as yer own idea.'

Jones began to see the humour of the situation. These cockneys certainly had the gift of the gab. He wondered if this sawn-off one had ever operated in Petticoat Lane.

He sniffed. 'All right, then, just this once I'll buy it — but it hadn't better be a leg-pull! Understand? Otherwise you'll be treated to an overdue bath, in the hogwash!'

'You're on, are yer?' Harris chortled. ''Ere's me 'and. Shake on it!'

The two of them shook hands. Harris turned and scampered up the beach. 'Stay right there, Cox'n! I'll be back!' he shouted over his shoulder.

Taff Jones hauled off his sweat-rimed peaked cap, and scratched at his close-cropped carroty hair. He felt certain the little Cockney would be back, but for the life of him he could not figure out what the bright idea was going to be.

He waited.

3

Lofty Rawson paced his bridge restlessly.

For once his habitual high spirits had taken a beating. All had gone well until they wanted to start back to Messina and then the perishing port engine had refused to start. P.O. Motor Mechanic Jock Dodd had been up to the bridge to report twice in the past two hours. His appearance had been almost laughable. His lined face had been so streaked with oil that he looked like a badly made-up nigger minstrel.

His language in the engine-room had been fit to turn the air blue.

Rawson was aware that his ship was a sitting duck. True, enemy air attacks had become few and far between, but it only needed one lucky shot — like the one which had exploded the ammo cases — and L.C.T. 17 would be just another battered hulk at her last resting place.

She was ugly, ungainly, badly planned

and very frustrating at times, but she was home to the fourteen worthy men who made up her crew. Aboard her they were a known team. If they had to go back to U.K. without her, it would mean another boring session of being pushed around in R.N.B., being separated, and perhaps being sent to a packet which was much worse.

Rawson paused in his heavy pacing.

Ten minutes ago the Beach Control Officer had been over to speak to him. He wanted the L.C. out of it. He had been rather short and snappy. Rawson had come perilously close to losing his temper and inviting the Control Officer on board to have a go himself. Fortunately, he had been able to restrain himself. What niggled him was the fact that almost all experienced naval officers who had not served in landing craft, didn't have the vaguest idea how difficult they were to handle.

To hell with him, thought Rawson. We must have another go! Just one more try to haul her into deep water with one engine playing up. He crouched over the engine-room voice-pipe.

'Jock, I'm going to make one more attempt, in about three minutes. Stand by!'

Dodd started to protest volubly, but Rawson replaced the cover on the pipe and walked away to the side of the bridge. He leaned out to starboard.

'Swain! Come abroad, we're going to try again!'

Jones trotted along the beach until he could see the skipper. 'Just hold on a minute, sir, will you? There's a chap ashore here thinks he knows how to get us off!'

Rawson thought: It sounds as if old Taff has met up with an Eyetie magician. But he called back, rather dejectedly: 'All right, man, but let me know what's going on as soon as you can!'

On the beach, Jones's eyebrows went up as Harris came back, trotting at the side of the bulldozer which they had ferried across. He was beginning to get an inkling of what the little cockney had in mind. Perched high in the driver's seat, the battered pug was grinning like a jackass.

'Better get them fags ready,' panted Harris.

Jones turned towards the ship, his hands cupped round his mouth. 'I think they're going to try and push us off with the bulldozer, sir!'

Rawson received the message in thoughtful silence. Presently, he rang down for both diesel engines to be started. 'All right, you take charge of that end, Swain!'

Jones acknowledged. He watched, fascinated, while Lewis ran the machine carefully up against the bow door. He had raised the great rammer so that its forward edge rested firmly against the slope of the bows.

'Ready when you are!' Lewis called, in his husky, gravelly voice.

'Any time now, sir!' Jones shouted.

The flat-bottomed ship vibrated as the revs in the starboard engine built up. Jones brought down his arm, and Lewis put his machine in gear. Harris threw himself to one side, hands protecting his face, as a twin shower of small pebbles flew backwards from under the caterpillars.

'Hold on . . . she's movin'!' bellowed Lewis, his voice pitched a tone or so higher than usual with excitement.

The curious faces of the crew peered down from the foc's'le, reflecting delight as the vessel eased backwards beneath them. Someone called: 'That bloke on the machine deserves sippers all round!'

Jones splashed slowly forward into the shallow water, following the receding bows. Behind him, Harris called out a reminder.

'There y'are, Cox'n! Don't you go thinkin' you got all the brains in the Senior Service! An' don't forget my packet of fags, either!'

Harris sounded anxious, Jones turned and waved to him. He shouted to a seaman in the bows, who went aft to get the cigarettes. The vessel was going astern to port when he got back with the packet. Harris watched anxiously as he threw the packet ashore. Jones caught it expertly, and threw it to him.

'There you are, mate,' he yelled, 'if ever you do a trip with us again you can drink my tot!'

'I'll keep yer to that, me old shiner!' Harris replied.

Jones was up to his knees in water by the time a Jacob's Ladder snaked down over the port bow to retrieve him. As he disappeared over the rail, the crew produced a ragged cheer. Rawson waved, and the vessel slowly turned itself about to head back for Sicily.

Lewis watched her, blinking hard. He held his cigarette cupped in the palm of his hand. At length, he turned to his small side-kick. 'Yer know, Nipper, this 'as been quite a day. I don't reckon I've enjoyed meself so much since I knocked aht old Bomber Wilson in the first round!'

An hour later, Scoop Britwell was standing in a wired compound occupied by over a hundred Italians of the coastal defence unit which had surrendered.

He had inspected for himself the shambles round the heavy calibre coastal weapons which were supposed to have rendered the Straits impassable. The gun-sites were completely devastated. Many of the forty-seven gun barrels had been knocked out of their foundations and had rolled down the slopes to the beaches like so many fallen logs.

In addition to reducing the guns to scrap metal, the naval squadron — headed by *Nelson* and *Rodney* had pulverised a barracks, an ammunition dump, and a radar station.

The attitude of the olive-skinned round-eyed Italian gunners round about him was difficult to understand. The average western European would have been completely deflated by the hammering they had received, but they were walking about, chatting volubly and cracking jokes one with another.

He knew sufficient Italian to be able to converse with them. They told him, with much hand gesticulation, that for them the war was over. They were glad to be finished. Although they were prisoners, they would wait patiently for the day when the Allies would drive the hated Bosche out of their beautiful land of sunshine for good!

When he mentioned Mussolini, they sniffed and spat on the earth. They cared nothing for him. The Allies could do their worst to him. All they wanted to do was get back to their womenfolk, raise families and drink lots of vino. What else could a man want they queried?

Presently, Scoop passed out of the compound, feeling self-conscious in the presence of the sentries when the Italians called after him cheerily, as though they had known him all their lives.

He wandered slowly through the shell-torn streets of the town, still wondering how the natives could feel so cheerful in such surroundings. Some of the older men had already gone back to their habitual siestas. He glanced down at them curiously, as they lay about, anywhere, snoring beneath broad-brimmed hats.

He was wondering about his future plans, when three laughing, chattering young girls intercepted him from a side turning. In a moment they were all over him, clinging round his neck, touching his damp shirt, patting his knapsack. He was forced to stop and speak to them.

For several moments they talked so quickly that he could not make out what they were saying. All he could pick out was the word *'Inglese'* which they repeated like a spell. Life stood still; it was a whirl of blue-black hair, flashing dark eyes and caressing fingers.

When he recovered from the shock, his first inclination was to shoo them away in his best pseudo-military manner. But he knew it would not work. Patiently, and not a little disturbed, he glanced at their weaving bodies as they plied him with grapes, nuts and oranges. Each of them had on a white peasant blouse, laced and wide at the neck, a skirt of darker material, and nothing else visible except a bright coloured apron.

He allowed himself to be kissed hard on the lips by the three of them in turn. Then the first one, who had a much more mature figure than the other two, started to haul her off her friends so as to monopolise him.

Angry expressions flashed across the faces of the other two, as the plump girl ordered them away, stabbing a determined forefinger in the direction from which they had appeared. Britwell caught his breath. His head had begun to reel with the intensity of their kissing. All of them had full red mouths, devoid — like the rest of their faces — of any signs of make-up.

The angry pair moved off slowly, protesting as they went. He stepped a pace or two clear of the determined one, but she turned sharply; reaching up with her hands to his shoulders. The movement showed him most of her olive breasts as he looked down at her. His eyes were tantalised. Her own dark eyes probed his own, as if assessing her own power to move him.

In slow, halting English, she said: '*Signore*, I am Amelita. I like the English. Amelita would like to be your girl. 'Ow would you like that?'

Her lush body remained pressed to his own. His sun glasses started to mist up. The girl smiled, showing a perfect set of teeth. Suddenly, she dropped one of her hands to the bunch of grapes he was clutching. Without taking her eyes from his own, she bit one in half and pushed part of it between his lips. Before he could protest, she had reached up and clamped her lips upon his. He felt the blood pounding through his veins.

Amelita's eyes rolled. A muted cry came out of her throat. With trembling hands he succeeded in separating their mouths. He was panting as she laced her fingers behind his head.

'*Signore*, I am not rich, but I am pretty. I have good body.'

Suddenly she freed herself, and pulled up her skirt revealing plump thighs which dimpled above the knees.

'You like me, eh?'

Britwell glanced round. Apart from sleeping bodies the place was deserted. But for the distant hum of lorries near the beach he could have imagined it all a dream.

Amelita moved closer again, pressing his hand to her breast. 'You take me away, now, I go anywhere. I am ready. You will not regret! If I am nice to you, you will take me to England, eh? Make me your wife. Amelita would like that!'

In spite of himself, Britwell caught her to him again. Her mouth opened under his like an open wound. Time stood still. Booted feet approached unnoticed. Wolf cries and whistles brought him back to the present. He looked up, startled. Moving towards him was a column of Canadian infantry, marching easily in threes.

A man in the front line shouted to him. 'Jesus, mate, that's a ripe one! Where did you pick her up?'

Another soldier turned to his officer, marching alongside. He said: 'Aw what the hell, Captain, why can't we fall out for half an hour? The Jerries'll wait for us to catch up!'

The officer's reply didn't carry to Britwell. The whole squad was laughing and calling out to him by now. He took a deep breath, tilted Amelita's head up to his own.

'Now see here, Amelita, you're a very sweet girl. You have a lovely body and — and everything, but I can't take you with me. I have a wife back in England, and — and six children. You see . . .'

Amelita pouted and was about to protest.

'You must find yourself a soldier who is not married,' he persisted urgently. 'Why don't you try one of those Canadians?'

She repeated the word 'Canadian' as though savouring it. An N.C.O. who was just passing them caught Britwell's last words. He said: 'Yeh, *signorina*, why don't you try one of us? We'll be glad to help you!'

The girl hesitated. Britwell pushed her towards them. 'Good luck,' he murmured, then *'arriverderci,'* wondering if he had pronounced it correctly. On impulse, the girl brushed her lips against his own once more, then she was off, dancing towards the Canadians on bare, dirty feet.

The N.C.O. grabbed her first. A tiny sliver of grape skin transferred itself unnoticed from her lips to his. Britwell moved off, grinning and blushing under his tan. As he turned a corner, he glanced back.

The column had slowed, and the flashing-eyed buxom girl was being kissed and passed on down the threes. Her squeals of laughter trilled above their deeper voices.

Britwell's hand shook a little as he absently fitted a cigarette into his mouth. He reflected: I'm glad none of my fellow correspondents were about to hear me lay claim to a non-existent wife and six kids.

★ ★ ★

Half an hour later, he was in the back of a lorry with a score of infantrymen, bumping over the rutted roads which led north through Calabria. On his knees he had a thick signal pad. He was writing in it assiduously with a pencil.

4

Not all the Allied forces invading Calabria came from the island of Sicily. Apart from the two divisions which crossed the Straits of Messina against comparatively light opposition, many other units came direct — and fresh — from North Africa.

On the day following the capture of Reggio, two large British destroyers were making their way from Tripoli with four hundred commandos on board. They were bound for a small township on the northern side of the toe of Italy called Bagnare.

The sea was rough and the wind blustery, but the élite soldiers stayed on the upper decks of the warships either taking the air, or putting in a little strenuous exercise the better to be fit for their coming ordeal.

Right forward on the foc'sle of the *Lightning*-class destroyer *Livid*, Captain Tufty Britwell and his old peacetime buddy, Sergeant Dipper Marsh, clung to the guardrail and ducked from time to time as clouds of chilly spray flew from the knife-edged bows in all directions.

Further aft, in the starboard waist, a group of some thirty men, including officers and N.C.O.'s were indulging in a session of catch-as-catch-can wrestling. On the other side of the vessel another squad of commandos were being initiated into the art of a popular naval game known as deck hockey. Frequent sharp excited cries drifted from this group to reach the pair on the foc'sle before the wind finally scattered the sound.

Britwell and Marsh watched the spectacle with growing interest. It was played by two teams of about eleven players each, with shinty sticks and a small tight roll of manilla rope which served as a ball. For obvious reasons, a real ball would have been useless. As it was, about every three minutes some player, with more enthusiasm than skill, lofted the 'ball' over the side. Each time this occurred, the ship's P.T.I. threw another one down on the deck.

Britwell wiped salt spray from his face, and turned to his friend, grinning: 'Well, Dipper, I don't know what you think about all this. It isn't quite what I expected of the Senior Service. They certainly seem to know how to amuse themselves at sea. I always thought it was all sleeping and watch-keeping when the ship was under way.'

Dipper Marsh ran thick fingers through his shock of dark wavy hair. He had a wide mouth like Joe E. Brown, and at this moment he grinned, stretching it from ear to ear.

'No, mate, you've got it all wrong. They give out things like that to keep the Andrew from getting overcrowded. Now, take my brother, Sam. He's been in the R.N. for twelve years, in fact he's just signed for the other ten. He's never taken any harm. A four-year commission in the Med, and another in South Africa. You can't beat it!' Marsh winked his left eye and tilted his head on one side. 'No, he wouldn't have changed with the likes of us in peacetime. And in wartime, there's no difference. We're here on the job just the same as he is, taking the same risks. If you ask me, there's a lot to be said for a wife in every port. Mind you, old Sam's single, and likely to remain so. I suppose that makes a difference.'

Britwell nodded. He remained silent for a moment, as though weighing up what Marsh had said.

This Britwell, the younger brother of Scoop, was much the same as the war correspondent in height. But he weighed nearly two stones heavier. His shoulders were much thicker and so was his trunk. He had a good head of fair hair like his brother. It was trimmed stiffly in a squarish crew-cut and the sun had not had the same chance to bleach it. His eyes were an identical shade of blue.

As Marsh rambled on about the advantages of a wife in every port, he was thinking of his own pretty wife back home in Shepherds Bush. And the twin two-year old babies she had borne him, Paul and Paula. Travel to the married man, he reflected could never be quite as carefree and exciting as bachelors made it out to be. With the married state there was always the home tie, pulling at a man's heart-strings drawing him home again. He supposed it was true that love could draw him further than gunpowder could blow him.

It stood to sense.

Marsh was the first to break the silence which had grown between them. He gripped Britwell by the shoulder, grimacing. 'D'you know, Tufty, I've got a queer sensation in my stomach. I know I'm not sickening for anything, but — '

'Seasickness, chum!'

'But I never been seasick in my life,' Marsh argued, his pride hurt.

'Just the same that's what it'll be,' Britwell insisted. 'Come on, let's get a bit further aft, where there's less motion.'

The two started aft off the foc'sle, keeping quite close to the guardrail. Like all other personnel they had uninflated lifebelts taped round their waists and over the shoulders. They would have felt more than a little sick if they had known the lifebelts would be needed before the day was out.

'Destroyers don't have the same motion

as larger ships,' Britwell was explaining.

'How do you mean?' Marsh asked soberly.

'Well, take a look at her. She's burying her nose and then her stern. Pitching and tossing, the mateloes call it. Now, if you think back to the trooper which brought us out here, and films you've seen of battleships and ocean liners, you'll see the difference. They're too big to pitch and toss — too long. Instead, they roll from side to side. I figure a chap could get used to one kind of motion and still be seasick when he first encountered the other.'

Marsh was impressed. He said: 'I believe you're right. In fact, I'm sure you are! You're a ruddy genius, Tufty, and no mistake. The Metropolitan Commissioners were on a sure thing when they recommended you for Hendon Police College. You'll end up a Commissioner yourself some day!'

Britwell shrugged off his friend's compliment. He smote him on the back. 'I vote we go down to the ward-room and try for a snack. What do you say, chum? They say a little food tends to steady a queasy stomach.'

Marsh readily agreed. He led the way below down the nearest deck hatch.

★ ★ ★

At 1600 hours, the commanding officer of H.M.S. *Livid* broadcast over the ship's Tannoy system to the crew and passengers. In every flat and passageway which sported a loudspeaker, they clustered eagerly, wondering what information he had for them.

His voice poured forth with the regular naval beginning.

'Do you hear there? This is the Captain speaking. Most of the ship's company will be aware by now that the four hundred men of the Home Counties Commando taking passage with *Launch* and ourselves are heading for Italy. What you don't know is their exact destination. It is a small port on the northern side of the toe of Italy, some miles ahead of the British Eighth Army which invaded Calabria successfully yesterday. Although not without their quota of casualties, the Eighth have made reasonable progress against a rapidly withdrawing enemy. The Italians in the area have already given in, but there are still some thousands of seasoned German troops who will put up a stout resistance as soon as the terrain starts to favour them.

'This stiffening of the resistance is expected to start in the Bagnare area, where there is a river mouth which will hold up pursuit. That is why Bagnare has been chosen for the Commando assault. If all goes well they should go in at dawn tomorrow. We are now a few miles south of the Messina Straits. That is all.'

As the speakers rattled and went dead, most off-duty men poured out on the upper deck for a breather and a smoke. They were just in time to hear an excited shout from the port lookout on the bridge.

'Enemy plane on the port bow, sir! On reconnaissance, by the look of it. Could be a Dornier!'

The guns' crews were immediately piped to action stations. Flags fluttered at the yard arm of the sister ship, which was lying astern. She also had noticed the snooper.

Livid acknowledged. The commandos peered up at the bridge curiously, seeking out the duffle-coated figure who had been addressing them over the Tannoy. He was issuing rapid orders. The crew of A 4″ mounting, situated forward of the bridge immediately went into their much-practised drill.

They presented an alert, exciting spectacle, in their overalls, lifebelts, anti-flash gear and tin helmets. Two minutes later, the first 4″ shell winged its way through the upper atmosphere towards the low-flying Dornier. It burst a full cable's length short in a grey mushroom of smoke. Another shell followed it quickly when the range had been adjusted, but again the projectile was short. The plane was making off, and keeping just out of range.

Firing ceased, and the watching sailors and soldiers saw it fly across the skyline ahead of them to take up station in a similar position wide of their sister ship.

A seaman with his white cap tilted

forward over his eyes was standing behind Britwell and Marsh. He spat expertly over the side. He grunted. 'They've got tabs on us now, any road,' he muttered. 'We can expect a spot of bother before nightfall.'

The two commandos exchanged glances. They were to remember his prophetic words later.

★ ★ ★

Dusk was making the closed-up gunners blink their eyes when the expected action came. One moment the sky was clear, and the next three Stukas were screaming in to the attack from a north-easterly direction.

The soldiers found it fascinating to watch them peel off at a great height, one at a time, and plunge into their dive. The first two headed for *Livid*, and the third dived at *Launch*.

Bells rang on the gun platforms. Gun captains warned their crews with hoarse shouts. Suddenly the scream of the diving planes was blotted out by the opening up of the guns. Four-inch, Oerlikons and pom-poms came to life in a flash. The darkening silhouette of the slim-lined vessel was thrown into relief by the streams of tracer which poured from it, and the orange-flamed back-lash of the larger calibred-weapons.

Through the leaden sky the tracers reached, groping and probing for the vitals of the plane. The bullets poured round it as it dived, like golden thread on a dark garment. To the dry-mouthed spectators, it appeared to have a charmed life. Lower and lower it dropped. Two bombs fell away from it. While the watchers discussed them in whispers, another pair were released.

A deadly pom-pom on the starboard side of the bridge was pushing its shells right down the pilot's throat. A gasp went up as the cockpit was wreathed in smoke. Flame dragged away from it, clutching with red elusive fingers at the fuselage. The plane slowed in its dive. It was going out of control.

With the bombs still falling towards them, nobody thought to cheer. Although the plane was stricken, the pilot might still have made his strike. The noise of the guns died, as the gunners stopped firing and probed the upper atmosphere for the new target. In the silence which ensued, soldiers and sailors alike held their breath.

The first stick of bombs was almost upon them.

They fell into the sea, raising twin gouts of water, mast-high, fifty yards from the starboard beam. A quick breath, and the next pair were with them, one exploding no more than five yards from the starboard side, and its twin actually scraping the guardrail on the port quarter.

The suspense was shattering during the mere second when it was expected that the bomb would explode. The second passed, it grew to five, and then ten. Men began to gasp like landed fish. After half a minute, a husky voice croaked:

'It ain't goin' to explode! Strike me, it was a dud! What are the Jerries comin' to? I'm goin' to take me shares out o' Krupps as soon as I gets back to U.K.!'

The stricken plane flew into a thousand fragments five hundred yards to port. The ear-shattering tinny rattle began again, as the guns lined up on the second Stuka. But this second pilot had no pressing need for an Iron Cross. He released his bombs, not too accurately, rather too high to do any damage. He dropped his starboard wing, eased back his control column, and headed back the way he had come in a beautiful arc. The navy gave him a throaty cheer, punctuated by many raspberries.

The gun crews got their breath, kicked their feet clear of the mountains of empty cases and squinted into the dusk to see how *Launch* had fared. Her adversary had tried honourably and missed. He was on his way home. The destroyer was unscathed.

The ship went into second degree of readiness.

Britwell and Marsh stayed on the upper when most of the commandos went below to turn in. They leaned over the guardrail, watching a couple of porpoises besporting themselves round the bows, and marvelling at the brilliant phosphorescence in the tumbling wave-caps.

'What do you make of that little lot, Tufty?' Marsh enquired. 'Short, sharp and nasty, if you ask me.'

'I couldn't agree more, Dipper. Down the London Underground is the safest place I know when that sort of caper starts. A funny thing, though. I was just thinking what a thrilling bit of reading the attack would have made in the old *Daily Globe*, if our Harry had written it up. He's a dab hand at racy descriptions.'

Marsh gave vent to Britwell's thoughts. He said: 'Talking of old Scoop, I wonder where he is now?'

5

Night cloaked the eternal blue sky of the Mediterranean like a dark velvet gown, sequined modestly with stars. The blustery wind which had sprung up in daylight, still prevailed, scything the caps of the black sea-mountains into clouds of biting spume.

Visibility was poor, and there was no indication that it was likely to improve quickly. Watch-keeping in warships at times like these was a lonely vigil. Staring through glasses with tired, raw eyes gave a man the impression that he was in another world. Even the ship in which he had his being seemed to have changed its identity . . .

$\star \quad \star \quad \star$

Britwell and Marsh had wisely turned in shortly after the dusk air attack. For a time, both of them had lain back on the

65

hammock mattresses which had been issued to them, marshalling their minds towards the morrow.

They were in an enclosed, petty officers' mess on the main deck. Unlike a broadside seamen's or stoker's mess, it had some privacy. Separating it from other messes, and the passage which flanked it inboard, were shiny polished lockers, two tiers high. Above the locker tops, and reaching to the moist deckhead were dark blue curtains which shifted slightly with the movement of the ship.

All the time there was a gentle protesting of metal as the destroyer's knife bows carved their way through the alien sea's troughs and ridges.

The mess was dimly lit by a single blue police-light, low on one bulkhead. It showed a score of hammocks, swinging gently near the deckhead a regulation eighteen-inches apart. Half of them were empty, their occupants doing a four-hour watch. The others cradled tired men who slept like rocked babes.

In every naval mess, there is always a small core of men who do not 'sling up' if they can possibly help it. In this mess, there were four of them. They lay on low, wide cushioned stools, on spread hammocks. In order not to be pitched off their precarious sleeping places, they lay on their sides, arms folded squarely across their chests, knees together and drawn up half way.

The commandos were on the deck itself. Britwell and Marsh had picked for themselves a cosy 'billet' inside the metal hammock rack, raised up from the deck on wooden laths. Both of them snored gently. They were as much at ease as the regular sailors.

Nobody was prepared for disaster when it came.

A tall, red-faced Lancastrian able-seaman, keeping watch as a starboard lookout on the bridge was the first man to know anything.

He panned round his night glasses for perhaps the fiftieth time during that watch, coming to a sudden stop, with mouth agape. Coming right towards him from the east was the unmistakable lighter track of a hostile torpedo.

He caught at his breath, blinked, and looked again, sweat starting out on his brow. Seconds later, he found his voice. Swinging round to shout over his shoulder, he called hoarsely: 'Tinfish on the starboard beam, sir!'

The silent figures on the bridge were galvanised into life. The navigator poked a pale, strained face out from his shrouded chart-room. The officer of the watch thumped across to starboard, fumbling at his glasses with mittened hands. Behind the binnacle, the captain — a tall man — took a quick spot check in the direction indicated.

Already his brain was racing to meet the emergency.

'Engine-room, Full Ahead, both! Maximum revs,' he called into one voice-pipe. And then into another: 'Helmsman wheel hard a-starboard!'

The key men in the engine-room and the wheelhouse echoed his words. The ship heeled over to port as the bows came round in a racing turn. The klaxon warning note sounded throughout the ship.

'Both watches of the hands, stand to!'

The passengers came awake sharply, more disturbed by the bodies dropping out of the hammocks than by the curt order over the broadcasting system. They knuckled their eyes and peered aghast at the hurrying, sleepy figures as they snatched up gas masks, lifebelts and anti-flash gear and disappeared.

Metal ladders everywhere clanged to the thump of racing sea-boots. Britwell and Marsh grabbed for the sides of the hammock rack to keep their feet.

Britwell said: 'I don't like this, Dipper!'

'That goes for me, too, mate,' Marsh answered, glancing around him apprehensively.

'Let's go out on the upper,' Britwell suggested.

The other commandos followed him without a word, grabbing their kit as they moved out. They were not to know, but the alarm had been sounded seconds too late to be of any use. They had reached the upper deck by the nearest hatch, and were cowering against the superstructure when the torpedo struck into the ship's vitals, well aft on the starboard side.

The vessel lurched. It listed further to port, lost momentum and straightened up, listing to an angle of forty-five degrees the other way. But this time the list stayed. The forty-five degrees became fifty. Great jets of steam started to hiss internally. A party of damage control workers scurried aft to size up the damage.

The passengers waited fearfully and wondered.

The ship slowed to a stop, wallowing slowly, getting deeper in the water. Crew and passengers alike were listening, not knowing quite what to expect. When the instruction came it was a relief, in a way.

'All personnel to abandon ship stations. On the double!'

Now the passengers could see the sense of the infinitely boring drill which had been carried out before the ship was out of sight of Tripoli.

A winking Aldis lamp message from the other ship gave them confidence as they scrambled down the sloping decks to their appointed places. Already a slick party of seamen were lowering the ship's motor launch into the plunging sea, instructed by the ship's cox'n.

Britwell and the handful of men with him waited dutifully as the launch sank lower. Half a dozen crates of small arms belonging to the Commandos were already stacked in it. They would still be useful for the assault, Britwell thought, provided the sea did not get at them. But what of the jeeps and the gun carriers?

He thought of querying the matter with the cox'n, but decided against it when a calm young sub-lieutenant arrived to make sure their evacuation was going according to plan.

'Everything all right, sir?' he asked briefly. 'You won't be long before the *Launch* picks you up. She's standing by already.'

'Don't worry about us, sub,' Britwell advised, 'I'm sure you've other worries!'

The officer went off, and while the launch was still dangling from the falls, Tufty had time for a quick glance round. The ships' boats were already lowered and manned. Small parties had cut down the Carley floats, dropped them in the sea and scrambled after them. From one of them the sound of laughter floated. A voice called out: 'This is better than the water-chute at Blackpool, Nobby!'

'You can spray that again, Scouse!' came the breathless reply.

Then Britwell and company were stepping cautiously over the rails and onto a swaying Jacob's Ladder. This was something they hadn't practised. A Jacob's Ladder can only be climbed one way, unless it is up against a ship's side. And this one was dangling in space.

A voice from a boat right forward added to the slight panic. 'Hurry it up, you chaps right aft! She's starting to slip!'

Me, too, Tufty thought, as the ladder swayed and reared away from him.

'Climb down the side of it, sir!' a voice bellowed from below. 'One foot one side, then the next one the other.'

Britwell tried it somewhat doubtfully and found it worked.

'Pull away there, motor launch!' called the same voice. 'You must get clear of the undertow!'

As willing hands hauled Britwell into the swaying launch, the men following him got the wind up. Marsh's clawing body sailed past him and landed with a splash in the drink, right alongside the launch. Before Britwell could get a word out, a boathook had been hooked into Marsh's lifebelt and he was being hauled out again.

Half a dozen men actually jumped into the sea, when they saw what had happened to Marsh. They, too, were hauled out quickly. The launch went astern, its bows came round and the engine raced to Full Ahead. All eyes were turned to *Livid*, making its last plunge. She slid away as gracefully as she had been in life, stern first. Up, and up still more came the bows. The smokestack disappeared amid creaming foam and billowing smoke. Then the bridge followed it. The sliding gained momentum. In half a minute she was under. A great spreading circular wave was being swallowed up, leaving only floating spars and small debris to mark her resting place.

Beyond the debris, a score of sailors,

swearing and grumbling in the sea, were held up by their lifebelts. Their boat, one of the port ones, had capsized as it slipped off the falls. From the other ship, they were the highlights of a truly macabre scene, as they bobbed up and down with their tiny red shoulder bulbs winking in and out among the waves.

★ ★ ★

H.M.S. *Launch* made a first class job of retrieving *Livid's* crew and passengers from what might easily have become a watery grave. Only two seamen and one commando were found to be missing at the check-up.

Launch kept to her course and orders at increased speed, while the commando officers held an emergency meeting in the captain's cabin. It was presided over by a rock-faced fifty-year old lieutenant-colonel with flinty eyes and dark tufts of hair sprouting from under his cheek-bones. Known as 'Old Granite' to his men, Colonel Hobbs was a noted mountain-climber. Thanks to his arduous hobby he had a tough body which would have looked well on men half his age.

Seated firmly in the Captain's swivel chair, he scrutinised the round dozen of officers sitting and standing around him. 'I know what you must be thinking, and I can't blame you. Having lost most of our jeeps and the gun carriers the odds against our making a profitable strike ashore are high against us. I want you to think it over.

'Our latest information is that the Eight Army is now temporarily halted, more by a demolished bridge over a river rather than by the enemy. They have captured Reggio, and the next town to it, San Giovanni. They can't afford to be held up long, otherwise the Germans will have time to regroup and make the push to Naples very arduous and costly.

'The Canadians cannot help them. As soon as Reggio fell, they moved off along the southern beaches, towards the instep, if you follow me. There is a range of sizeable hills between the two Allied forces. I still think it is imperative that we go in at dawn, and hit the enemy hard.

After this rough night, they can hardly be expecting another sea-borne assault so quickly. Now, what do you say?'

In turn, the whole group signified their approval of the Colonel's decision to go on.

The old man beamed. From his squatting position beside the cabin door, Britwell half raised his right hand.

'Well, what is it, Britwell?'

'About the transport, sir,' the captain prompted.

'Yes, of course. Let's deal with the problem of getting ashore first. We still have enough assault canoes for a score of men to go in close, as planned. The beaches, we are hoping, will not have been prepared for us. Any of you want to volunteer for the canoe work?'

Britwell and a young subaltern got their hands up a fraction before the others. Their fellow officers chaffed them, and then the business proceeded.

'The rest of us will go in with the collapsible dinghies and a small collection of rafts, which the skipper has put at our disposal. Some of you will have already noted their efficiency.'

Another ripple of laughter went round the group. The colonel took time out to stoke his pipe. When it was going well, he resumed.

'Now, as to transport ashore, when we want to move on. This, I think, was what Britwell had in mind. Of course we can't just hang about in a place we've taken, hoping against hope that the infantry will give us a lift now and then. That would be beneath an élite of soldiery such as we are.

'No, I have a better idea. We must make our sortie so effective that we take everyone by surprise — catch them with their pants down, as the Yanks say. Now, that won't be easy, not with Italians. We've seen in North Africa how keen they are to move out when things start getting a bit hectic. They'll be straining at the chocks, so to speak, as soon as the first angry shots are fired. One thing we can be certain of, if they're going to run, they'll have the wherewithal with which to evacuate. In other words, plenty of transport handy.'

The colonel squinted down at his pipe, tapped the tobacco a little, and blinked.

'You're aiming to steal their transport, Colonel?' a quiet major thoughtfully suggested.

'How right you are Ennis! We steal theirs. It's the thing we would be expected to do, as commandos! Don't you agree, the rest of you?'

The solid wall of enthusiastic comment left him in no doubt of their agreement. As the tiny cabin, with scuttle and deadlight closed, gradually filled up with wisps of tobacco smoke, the plan was thrashed out, detail by detail. Gaps of silence in the discussion were becoming more frequent when a small loudspeaker on the wall crackled into life. The officers broke off, peering up at it curiously.

They eyed one another with growing excitement, as a thin, west-country bos'n's mate made his announcement. His voice was pitched unmelodiously a little lower than his whistle.

He chanted: 'Heave-O, heave-O, heave-O . . . All the morning watchmen . . . *turn out*!'

The colonel rose to his feet. 'That's a reminder to us,' he said. 'Have your men assembled on the upper in half an hour. Britwell, the canoe squad will be in the starboard waist. Good luck to all of you. See if you can get your hands on a few bottles of Chianti when you get ashore. I'm rather partial to it.'

The party broke up in good order.

6

Ten minutes after five o'clock, ten lean canoes, each bearing three men, steadily widened the already promising gap between the shadowy silhouette of H.M.S. *Launch* and the shore.

Tufty Britwell sat in the back of the foremost canoe. He had a Sten gun cradled across his body. Pinned to the back of his shirt was a luminous circle of canvas to guide those who came after. From time to time, he glanced back. All the crews were pulling well and making steady progress.

In front of Tufty, Sergeant Marsh and another man, Private Rigg, pulled steadily with double-ended paddles. Rigg, immediately in front of Britwell, burped loudly. He had a phenomenal appetite. His burping was quite frequent, and as a result he had the nickname of Windy.

'Surely we don't have to have that row now,' Britwell grumbled, 'you'll give the alarm, if you aren't careful.'

Rigg muttered something unintelligible. Britwell ignored him, and ran his eyes round the shoreline which was rapidly becoming more distinct. Back from the beach, the town of Bagnare was fitted into the side of a hill. It was quiet now. Only an occasional puff of fluted smoke from a cottage chimney betrayed signs of life.

Further to the south it was different. Some three miles away, presumably in the San Giovanni area, unwanted fires which had burned all night were now dying down. Britwell thought about that. He wondered if any of the retreating German Panzers were bivouacked in Bagnare. It would be difficult to tell before they were actually ashore.

The bright line of phosphorescence along the beach fringe was no more than a hundred yards off by now. He trained his glasses on the shingle, and saw to his satisfaction that there was no sign of barbed wire. With luck there would be no mines about. About two hundred yards up the beach, however, he could see quite clearly a pair of hexagonal pill-boxes with several slits at head level facing the sea. The sides of the boxes were painted in zig-zag camouflage patterns, and large nets, sprouting tree branches and leaves, made them seem rather grotesque.

From one of the slits pointing north, a thin sliver of horizontal white light shone down the beach, and a melodious, muted tenor voice carried to him, singing a snatch of Puccini in Italian.

He grinned. Italians were less alert than Germans. Perhaps the going would not be too hard. Without turning round, he raised his right arm and flapped it up and down for the benefit of the others, like a motorist might do.

'No more talking, or burping, from now on,' he murmured.

Three minutes later the bow rubbed on shingle. Marsh hopped out and lowered his face veil. He held the canoe steady while the others scrambled clear. Shipping the paddles, they gripped their weapons firmly and hefted the canoe out of the water, walking forward with it until they were about ten yards from the water's edge. There, they put it down and briefly inspected each other. Puccini still carried to them, rising and falling with the singer's ebbing-and-flowing early morning enthusiasm.

Britwell blinked, thinking to himself that this was his most important sortie to date. And these two men beside him were those who would share his death, if they were spotted too soon. Marsh and Rigg had blackened their faces under the veils. Old man Britwell would have said they were pessimists, taking double precautions. But this was no time for nostalgia.

Britwell stuck up his thumb. The others followed suit. He pointed briefly at the pill-box to their right, and then flopped silently to the shingle, sniffing anew the salty tang, and wondering if the seaweed there would make anyone sneeze. Behind him, as he started to wriggle forward, he could hear the other boats quietly grounding. He did not turn round, in case his luminous spot showed in the wrong direction.

Ten minutes later, he and his two companions stopped, not more than five yards away from the box. They waited two minutes, regaining their breath, and such was the tension at this stage that each man counted off the seconds on his luminous wrist-watch.

Britwell turned his head towards them and nodded. He rose like a wraith, and slowly started forward, grounding his feet with extreme care. When he reached the door, he carefully poised himself, flexing his muscles, shifting the Sten from his left, and working his right arm like a tired barman. He tried the door. It was locked. As he tried it the singer inside suddenly erupted into song once more. For a moment, he thought he had been discovered. But no scampering feet crossed to the door. No rapid-firing machine-gun perforated it, and him.

He breathed deeply, feeling cold perspiration break out on his brow. His brain was racing. He would have to try and trick the man inside, if he was to gain entry without giving the alarm. The others were beside one of the front walls now, crouched under the slit. There was no time to lose. Any moment, one of them might inadvertently give the game away by making a noise. He wondered if his Italian would be proof against the conversation which must take place.

He knocked, quietly. The singer stopped in the middle of an aria. 'Who is there?'

Britwell made a shushing noise. He whispered: 'Is Bruno there?'

The singer yawned. 'Bruno? Who's Bruno? We've no Brunos here. Try the other pill-box.'

Britwell hesitated a moment, then he tried again.

'Look here, there's a bunch of Germans prowling around, looking for trouble. Let me in, will you? I won't disturb you for long.'

A round Latin oath floated out of the pill-box over the heads of the crouching pair. The man inside became impatient. He crossed to the door with short, sharp steps and threw it open. Before he could speak, Britwell seized him by the throat with his left hand. The man was no more than five-feet three in his stocking feet. The grip on his throat lifted him clear of the ground and bore him back inside.

In the dim light from a shrouded lamp, Britwell could see his face purpling, his tongue swelling and lolling out. He lowered him quietly to the ground where he lay like a sack, making quiet little noises like a dog with a bone in its throat.

Also in the box were five sleeping Italians, in two-tiered bunks round the back walls. Marsh and Rigg slipped in. On their feet they had socks over their boots. They left a wet trail. Britwell motioned for them to keep an eye on the sleepers. He stepped to a slit facing the sea, and took out his torch. Resting it on his left forearm, he flashed a message to those who followed. Dawn was breaking in the east. The fading darkness would not afford cover for very much longer.

Seventeen more men wriggled up the shingle towards the box without a sound.

Britwell lit a cigarette and waited for them. Besides the weapons and bunks, there was a table in the box. On it were Two empty Chianti bottles. A third was half full. He thought of the colonel and grinned.

Marsh sat at the table, his Bren handy

to menace anyone who showed wakefulness. Rigg moved to another gun slit which opened on the side nearest the other pill-box.

One after another, the men of Britwell's stick tiptoed into the box. He paid no attention, watching all the while for signs of further craft making their way inshore. Dinghies and rafts would be slower than the canoes. But the men could see the sky breaking as well as he could.

He felt as though he were sitting on a gunpowder keg with a slow-burning fuse. One of the last-comers trussed the singer, who showed signs of recovery. Just as he thought all was going well, an outcry broke out in the next pill-box.

His heart fluttered. Something had almost certainly gone wrong. When he spoke he found it a relief to be able to raise his voice.

'Two of you truss that lot! Marsh, you, Rigg and six more follow me to the other box!'

He ran from the box and sprinted breathlessly across the intervening shingle.

A long-barrelled gun was firing through one of the front slits. Shells were pitching round a small flotilla of Carley rafts. Even as he glanced seawards, one of them capsized and another was hit.

Fumbling for the grenades at his waist, he slid two into his left hand. He rolled them around, barrow-boy fashion, till the pins were uppermost and together. Then he ducked, still running, under the slits and flattened out against the front wall, straightening slowly. All was not yet lost! If only he'd tackled the second box earlier . . .

He pressed the grenades to his face, bit out the pins with his teeth and spat them clear. The first grenade he thrust through the slit where the gun was firing. The second, he rolled through the one next to it. Ducking again, he ran round to the door, holding onto it in case anyone tried to get out.

He had a glimpse of his eight men, ringing the box from the rear, guns ready before the first exploded, immediately followed by the second. The box appeared to shudder. He stepped back a pace, counted three and hit the door with his shoulder. It gave easily. Wreaths of acrid smoke poured out at him.

As he pushed his way through it, it occurred to him that he was taking a sizeable risk. But he did not hesitate. Of the six men manning the box, all had died except two who had been sheltered when the table went over. One of them, surprisingly, still showed fight. He was bringing up an automatic weapon when Britwell silenced both of them with a short burst from the Sten.

'Everything's under control here!' he barked, and then he began to cough. He stepped out again, leaving the door open.

'Marsh, you stay by me. Rigg and the rest of you get over by those trees and keep a sharp lookout for any support coming from the town!'

The others went off to do his bidding while he flashed another message seawards. In a matter of minutes, scores of men were walking up the beach. Their expressions were grim. Two of them carried a slack burden between them. Britwell went forward to hear the worst.

The news came as a profound shock to him.

'It's the colonel, sir,' a private told him. ''It in the abdomen. Lost a lot of blood.'

He glanced down at the familiar face, racked with pain. The eyes flickered open. 'What — what the hell are you looking so peeved about, Tufty?' the colonel murmured. 'I got in the way, not you. Did you find that Chianti I asked you about?'

Britwell shook himself, trying hard to concentrate.

'Chianti?' he repeated automatically. 'Oh, oh yes, I found half a bottle, sir.'

'Then take me to it!'

Tufty lit a cigarette, and thrust it between the Colonel's lips. He relieved the man at his head and helped carry the C.O. towards the first pill-box. He was thinking: If any bloke's drained that bottle, I'll murder him!

★ ★ ★

Within half an hour, German 88mm. guns had opened up on the beach from a point on a hill further north. But this did not trouble the Commando unduly. What seemed more ominous was the rumble of Tiger tanks coming up the coast road from the south.

It was time they dug themselves in somewhere. In a position where they could menace the tanks when they came closer. They would have to dig in on the hills above the town. Most of the officers and men moved off into the hills without pause. Britwell and his party took it upon themselves to look for the transport they would need if they were to move on.

An old peasant, one of the few natives to show himself, led them to a group of buildings back from the road. He showed them a dozen 3-tonners, Lancias, which were just what was required.

Britwell gave the old man a packet of cigarettes. He thanked them profusely and sat down outside the buildings, pulling the tobacco out of the cigarettes to stuff in his pipe.

'Now look here, chaps,' Britwell said, as he mopped his face and neck. 'We've found the transport, but we've got to hang on to it. It's just possible that the

Jerries coming up from the south might take a fancy to it. My idea is that we stay close, out of sight, just to make sure.'

'I'm with you, sir,' Marsh replied formally. 'I don't think the Jerries will rest long here. Our mob have lugged those Italian Bredas up the slope. They'll use them to good effect as soon as the tanks get near enough. They'll be only too glad to hurry on through.'

'How do the rest of you feel?'

There was general agreement. The men went to earth, in the trucks and in the tiny attics overhead. They spread out, cleaning their guns, smoking and chatting about the way the assault had gone, and the disturbing happenings when the destroyer had been sunk the night before.

Only Britwell and Marsh remained busy. They dug around until they found a large pot of red paint. Slapping it on roughly, they painted a huge red cross on the cab of the first Lancia. It was to serve as an ambulance for the colonel as soon as the route to the south was clear of the enemy.

At that moment, he was in the bed of

the same old man who had showed them the wagons.

'Do you think he'll be safe there, for the time being?' Britwell queried anxiously.

'As safe as in his own bed,' Marsh assured him. He added: 'And that old Eyetie woman has a touch like a mid-wife. He'll enjoy it!'

7

During the forty-eight hours after the commando assault on Bagnare, German resistance gradually stiffened up the west coast. Raids by the Luftwaffe against the Eighth Army became more and more prevalent.

Road blocks and demolished bridges made the advance painfully slow. At the end of this period of time, the engineers were just putting the finishing touches to the Bailey bridge in the river gorge, north of San Giovanni.

The Lancia truck, now being used as an ambulance, was the first vehicle to cross the improvised bridge in a southerly direction. It rolled into San Giovanni a little after midday, at the tail end of another German air attack, and bore its wounded officer straight to a primitive, one-storey hospital at the rear of the town.

Scoop Britwell, who was keeping close

to the bridge, hoping to win a lift to the north, stared at the Lancia with interest. As the Eighth Army spearhead troops did not appear to be leaving immediately, Scoop decided — on a hunch — to see what he could find out from the Lancia's occupant.

Having made up his mind, he followed it to the hospital and talked with the matron. His appearance did not impress her, but his careful Italian appeared to amuse her. Instead of dismissing him without hope, she mellowed a little.

'*Signore*, you do not seem to understand,' she protested, 'the officer has been wounded. He needs a blood transfusion. He is weak now. It is two days since he was laid low.'

Britwell waved his hands, Latin fashion. 'I wouldn't want to do anything to aggravate his condition, *Signora*, but — well, anything he could tell me might help the war effort. Help us to get the Germans out of Italy more quickly.'

'*Sì, sì*, I understand, but the only thing I can suggest is that you come back this afternoon. The doctor is with him now. I dare not disturb him.'

That was her last word. Her impressive receding figure reminded him of a large blue tea-cosy.

★   ★   ★

Mid-afternoon, he was back again, the worse for three glasses of wine and a growing sense of frustration. To his surprise, on application at the reception desk, he was conducted down a corridor without delay.

At the door to a small private ward, the matron materialised again. 'You may see him for ten minutes, *Signore*, the doctor has said. But no longer!'

She opened the door, ushered him inside, and went out again, closing it after her. The face of the man in the bed, although weathered, looked like parchment. Suspended on a frame beside him was a bottle of blood. A rubber tube led from the bottle to a bandage round his right bicep. The bottle was emptying a drip at a time.

The patient spoke first. 'Take a seat,

Mr. Britwell, and tell me how the invasion's going.'

Scoop blinked in surprise, took off his sun-glasses and sat down on the far side of the bed.

He grinned. 'You know me, sir?'

Hobbs twitched one cheek. 'I do. I'm Lieutenant-Colonel Hobbs, Home Counties 3rd Commando. Your brother is one of my officers. I like him a lot.'

'But, how did you know me, sir?'

'The matron described you to me,' Hobbs explained, with a dry chuckle. 'The description she gave you fitted the one I'd had previously from your brother, Jack.'

Scoop said: 'I see. How — how is Jack, Colonel?' As soon as he had spoken, he felt ill-at-ease. Etiquette would have had him enquire about the colonel first. He glanced at the blood bottle, betraying his thoughts.

'Oh, don't worry about me, son. I'll pick up just as soon as I've got a few pints of red stuff back in my veins. You haven't a fag on you, have you?'

Scoop lit one for him. When he was

settled again, the colonel said: 'Jack was fit and well when I left him early this morning. Most of my boys are up in the hills behind Bagnare. They knocked hell out of a column of tanks retreating north, day before yesterday!'

'And Jack is with them?' Scoop prompted gently.

The colonel did not bother to remove the cigarette from his mouth. He talked with it bobbing up and down.

'As a matter of fact, he's not. You see, on the way over we lost most of our vehicles when a destroyer was sunk. After leading the assault up the beach, Jack took it upon himself to seek out some Italian lorries — I came down here in one. Well, then we heard the Panzers pulling north towards us. Most of our chaps dug themselves in on the hills overlooking the road, but Jack took it upon himself to stay down in the town and keep an eye on the Lancias.

'He may be still there, or he may not. You see, the Germans started a formidable counter-attack from the north. He may have had to leave the town and take to the hills like the others. It's hard to say.'

'Why, that's wonderful news. I've been trying to contact him on and off for years,' Scoop explained. 'He's my only close relative, you understand.'

'He's one of my best officers,' the Colonel observed.

'If I went north with the Eighth spearhead, do you think I could get right through to him, sir?'

'It's very doubtful, son. When they slipped me away, the Germans had already retaken the lower end of the town. And reinforcements were still arriving. No, I'd say it'll take another day or so before the Eighth connect up with my boys.'

When Scoop heard this, he became thoughtful, sorting out and discarding short-term plans for moving himself further north. The colonel took his turn at asking questions. The newspaper man answered him fully and politely, but the ten minutes soon came to an end. Scoop rose when the matron arrived.

He shook the colonel's left hand.

'A boy scout handshake,' the colonel

chuckled, 'I wouldn't like to estimate how long it is since I did that before.'

Scoop thanked him for the interview, and the kind things he had said about Jack.

'I know what you have in mind, and I hope you catch up with him, son. But if you take my advice you'll give the coast road a miss.'

Britwell promised to act on the advice. He left grapes, walnuts and almonds from his pack, and followed the matron back to the entrance. Half an hour was long enough to ascertain that there were no ships moving north from the locality.

He bought more fruit and nuts, filling his pack, and all the while urging himself to a decision. It had to be the hills. In September the Italian summer was getting well on, but the sun was still very hot throughout the day and the prospect of climbing about eight hundred feet on foot with the sun on his back daunted him a little.

He dozed for an hour in the corner of a quiet vineyard, and then set off up a goat track.

The track was narrow, winding, and treacherous with loose stones washed into view and loosened by the rains. There were no signs of human feet upon it. As he climbed, he concentrated on his footwork, anxious not to throw his ankle.

About every fifteen minutes, he paused and looked back the way he had come. Through gaps in the trees he could see the Eighth Army vehicles slowly making their way north up the winding coastal road. The distant staccato chatter of machine-guns and the thump, thump of small field weapons broke the growing silence. The war seemed to be many miles further north.

On the beach at San Giovanni, now dropping far to his rear, two L.C.T.s were beached, bow doors open. At that distance they looked like whales stranded in a storm. Human activity near them was negligible.

He trained his glasses out to sea, and there he saw a small squadron of cruisers and destroyers patrolling the calm waters some eight or ten miles off-shore. From time to time a group of Allied planes flew north-easterly from Sicily to attack the railways and marshalling yards further north. Some two-hundred and fifty miles up the coast the first port of any size, Naples, was located.

All his training and experience told him that Naples would play a vital part in the Allies advance up the leg of Italy. It was the only port south of Rome from which a major offensive could be launched. Would the Allies be content to fight their way slowly up the coast road until they reached Naples? He thought not. There were far too few Allied troops fighting in Italy for that. So far as he knew, there were only two divisions backed up by commandos and American rangers.

Some other force would have to come from the sea. He wondered when, and where. He thought of Naples as it had been when he saw it last, in 1938. He had been sent by the *Daily Globe* on that occasion to try and interview an international criminal extradited from the United States.

Then, Naples had been beautiful. It had lived up to the legends about it. He thought of the saying: 'See Naples and Die!' His thoughts became more morose. Many Allied servicemen would die before they reached the fabulous port. And many more would lose their lives before the big push to the north took place from there. For them, the saying would come true.

He wondered if it would come true for himself; and more important than that. Whether it would come true for his brother, Jack. His expression softened. Dear old Jack! Looking after Jack had become the most important part of his life since their parents had died as the result of an accident in Southend.

He remembered him in his first pair of long trousers, a growing schoolboy at Marylebone Grammar School. And then in his first job as a dogsbody in the *Globe* offices. At long last he had been old enough to join the Metropolitan Police. Since joining the force he had never looked back. Hendon Police College had put him on the way to quick promotion. When the war claimed him he was a sub-station inspector with a bright future.

He had a flat in Bayswater Road, a pretty wife, and twins! He chuckled when he remembered that made him an uncle, twice over.

His thoughts were still in this pleasant vein when he heard the click of the weapon. He looked up ahead, startled. Five yards above him, off to his right, a tall German soldier had a machine-gun trained on his head. From the place where Britwell stood, rooted to the spot, he could see right along the barrel to the pale unblinking blue eyes on either side of the jutting Roman nose.

'*Halte!*' The voice was high-pitched and deadly.

He was a bit late with the command, though, thought Britwell as the sweat began to cement his cap to his forehead. For several seconds they eyed each other. Other Germans showed up ahead, more curious than startled. Finally the barrel of the weapon waved and he was invited to step off the path into a clearing. Upwards of a score of men had been lying on the ground, reconnoitring the coast road and beaches from which he had come.

He stepped among them, closely watched by the man with the gun. His hands were clapped firmly on his head. He felt a complete and utter fool. This was one time when *Our Man at the Front* had overdone it. Very likely he had sent his last despatch in for this war. And just when he was getting on the track of old Jack!

The Germans started to discuss him. A squat, mean-looking *feldwebel* stepped forward; he walked round Britwell eyeing him up through steel-rimmed spectacles.

He said to the man who had captured Britwell, in German: '*Gott in Himmel*, Wilhelm, what is this you have found?'

The soldier, Wilhelm, threw back his head in a sneering laugh. He replied: 'A stupid pig of an *Englander*. I could have shot him down and fifty more besides him. I think he is blind behind those green glasses.'

Britwell looked him over. He had understood almost literally all that had been said so far. The man's eyes were overbright and his nostrils twitched. He could not have been a day over twenty-three. A product of the Hitler Youth, for sure. The Hermann Goering armband suited his smirking face and overbearing attitude. Here was a killer, without a doubt. One who would take pleasure in it.

Anger crowded caution out of Britwell's mind. He peeled off his sun-glasses without haste and pushed them into his shirt pocket. While all around him goggled, he forced himself to smile at the cocksure Wilhelm.

'You're an arrogant, stupid pipsqueak of a Nazi nincompoop,' he said, slowly and deliberately in his best North Thames English.

The *feldwebel* stiffened, and the blond soldier turned to him, eyes flashing with suspicion, his brow clouded. To Britwell's intense surprise, the *feldwebel* repeated every word he had said. He had understood it all.

A wave of hostility spread around the assembled Germans. They looked from Wilhelm to the *feldwebel*, from Britwell to Wilhelm again. The blond man let out his breath in a long hissing snarl. He dropped the machine-gun at his feet and walked forward, eyes blazing. When he was no more than five feet away, he sprang forward, aiming a savage right-handed haymaker at Britwell's head.

Britwell rolled forward from the hips, allowed the blow to sail over his head. Then he straightened, catching the man by the shoulders, off-balance. *I'll give the bastard non-combatant*, he was thinking angrily. Throwing forward his right leg, he heaved the other backwards over it, letting go suddenly.

Wilhelm's own cry of rage was drowned by surprised voices of the others. He landed about eight feet away, slithered another yard, and pulled up on his haunches. One man, back in the group, emitted a sudden chuckle, which sounded louder because the others were silent again.

Evidently Wilhelm was not universally popular. There was no mistaking his intention when he scrambled back up the slope. Nobody sought to stop him as he scooped up his weapon again. He juggled it quickly across his chest and sighted it on Britwell's body. Scoop waited, riveted to the spot, seeing the index finger tighten on the trigger as though in slow motion.

The next few seconds were not quite clear to him until several hours later.

Just as the man was about to fire, a high-pitched shout of command came from the trees up the track. The watching men stiffened. The *feldwebel* swung up his foot. He kicked the barrel of the machine-gun to the marksman's right, just as he fired. As it was, the first two bullets clipped a furrow of skin from the Englishman's left forearm as the weapon swung off-target. The burst finished in little more than a second. Everyone turned to the young *Oberleutnant* who hurried towards them, his face a mask.

Wilhelm lowered the weapon and the *feldwebel* came to attention as he strode through them. He paused in front of Britwell, looking him over with dark, brooding eyes, which took in everything, including the shoulder flashes.

He nodded, turned to Wilhelm and gave him a look which appeared to shrivel him. He said to him one word: '*Schwein!*'

Then he turned to the *feldwebel* and gave him an order.

'Fall the men in, and bring the prisoner along with us. We'll interrogate him later.'

Britwell stumbled off with his hands secured behind his back. When some of the panic had left him, he thought, I wonder if the bastards are taking me north?

8

In addition to the shortage of seasoned troops available for the invasion of Calabria, the Allied High Command had another pressing problem which in no way eased during the Italian campaign. This was a serious shortage in the number of landing and assault craft. As a direct consequence, the L.C.T.s and smaller vessels which were on the spot, found themselves working a round-the-clock shuttle service, not only between Sicily and the mainland, but also between one point on the mainland and another further to the north.

Selected units of the invasion troops, in fact, were beach hopping. It left the Navy with little time for rest or recuperation.

L.C.T. 17 was one of the shuttle boats.

After being stuck on the beach at Reggio with a defunct port engine, the bearded skipper had insisted on twenty-four hours in Messina for an emergency repair. But such was the chaos in that overworked port, that it fell to the lot of Petty Officer Dodd to do the repair job himself, assisted by a couple of stokers who were scarcely interested.

One of the stokers, in fact, had the bright idea that if he mucked the job about a bit, the whole ship's company could loaf their time away in Sicily until some other so-and-so finished off the Italian campaign for them. When the job had dragged to forty-eight hours, the irate Naval-Officer-in-Charge had sent for Rawson. In spite of not being able to offer reasonable repair facilities he thought it his duty to give him a stiff telling-off about not having his boat fit for service.

Rawson spoke up for himself, rather forcefully, but he got out of the office quickly before the Commodore could start talking in terms of a court-martial.

Back on board ship, the glowering Scot had reported his malingering stoker, who had been threatened with an immediate draft chit if he didn't pull his weight. The threat did the trick. L.T.C. 17 left harbour at dawn the following day bound for Bagnare.

There, on the beach where they had made their assault, Rawson found Captain Britwell, a handful of officers and N.C.O.s and no more than half the original number of commandos wearily waiting to be taken off.

With storage space constructed for only four tanks and their crews, there was no room for the captured Lancias which Britwell had hoped to take along with them. As it was, about one hundred and eighty men had to take passage in the well-deck, which soon was as hot as the Black Hole of Calcutta, even with the canvas awnings rigged.

Rawson closed his bow door and eased out to sea again without mishap. Tufty Britwell had thankfully subsided into his own canvas chair in the forward port angle of the bridge. His full face was etched with lines of weariness which made Rawson hesitate to ask him how the fighting was going. Presently, however, the salty breeze had the effect of reviving Tufty, and Rawson took his chance.

'You been ashore in Italy for long, Captain?' he ventured.

Britwell grinned. He glanced appreciatively at Rawson's full set of whiskers and fingered his own stubbly chin.

He said: 'Four days, just over. Since then, we've been hanging on, waiting for the Eighth to catch up with us. They got through yesterday, but before they arrived, the Jerries counter-attacked in force from the north. It took us until last night to persuade them to pull out north again. By jove, I was pleased when we turned out this morning and found they'd pushed off! I was beginning to think we'd be bogged down there forever.'

Rawson nodded. He pulled off his battered peaked cap and hung it on the binnacle. The breeze started to ruffle his thinning hair. He produced a packet of cigarettes, put one in his mouth and threw the packet over to Britwell. While he was lighting his, the skipper turned round, eyeing his deck personnel somewhat critically. The messenger was crouched in a corner, very brown in blue-piped vest and white shorts working vigorously on a bucket of dhobeying. One lookout was tossing bits of ship's biscuit in the sea for an acrobatic gull which would have done well in a circus. The other had the horizon pin-pointed in a fixed stare as though he had just spotted Betty Grable with a mermaid's tail.

'Keep your eyes skinned, lads!' Rawson suggested.

He took a quick look round through his own glasses, saw nothing worth pondering over and let them dangle. He left the binnacle, arching his back and coming to rest with his bulk resting on the windbreak by his guest.

'Excuse me for mentioning it, Captain, you remind me very strongly of a bloke who took passage with us to Reggio. A very unusual chap, name of Britwell — war correspondent.'

'My brother, Harry!' Tufty beamed with pleasure. 'So the old joker's got himself in the thick of it again, has he? I'm glad you've met him, Skipper. How was he looking?'

Rawson grinned. 'I'm Rawson. Lofty to you. Your brother looked a bit browned off, I'd say — maybe a bit tired with the Sicily schemozzle. But we had quite a chat. He mentioned you. Said he was on the lookout for you. I took quite a fancy to him.'

Britwell warmed under the influence of Rawson's bluff charm. He started to talk freely. 'Been like a father to me, Harry has, since our old folks snuffed it. Before the war, you know, he was a crime reporter. And I for my sins was a Metropolitan policeman. Harry used to get tips from noses I never knew existed. He passed them on to me, and quite often I could make a tidy clean-up. Helped me to impress the top brass when I wanted promotion. Oh yes, I owe a lot to Harry.'

The conversation lasted for over half an hour. At the end of it, both men felt more relaxed, as though the war had been switched off for a while.

Rawson had a nose for coincidence. He thought how coincidental it was to meet two brothers, to give them both passage in his ship, within so short a time of each other. He thought they were both top-notchers, the type of chaps you could hope to see again, after the war, in civvies.

He wondered if that would ever happen, and what the odds were against it happening.

The war made itself known to them again without much warning. It took the shape of six high-flying Heinkels, heading from the large airport at Foggia, and bound apparently for Calabria.

Rawson gave the warning without need of artificial aid. Dhobeying buckets, paper-backed novels, love letters disappeared as if by magic. Tin hats, lifebelts and anti-flash gear were quickly in evidence. Ever since the invasion began, Rawson had been without his first lieutenant. The Subby, as he was known to all on board, had been shipped to North Africa for an appendix operation the day before the Allies crossed the toe.

As action loomed close again, Rawson wondered fleetingly how Sub-Lieutenant Smith was faring. He was a better shot than anyone on board with a two-pounder pom-pom . . .

'Stand by, lads!'

Thirteen pairs of anxious eyes watched the two flights of Heinkels moving smoothly across the sky. Somebody said: 'Uh-huh,' as the second group altered course so as to fly over the ship.

Rawson banged his engine-room telegraph to *Full Ahead, Both*. He called down a warning to his motor mechanic. Jock grunted without answering.

Six bombs tumbled towards them like confetti.

'Hard a-port, Jonesy!'

The unwieldy craft swung through a wide arc, punishing the waves in its path. Down below the huddled soldiers muttered and cursed. A quick glance round the horizon showed there was no other ship in sight to back them up. They were for it.

'The other three are keeping on course,' Tufty breathed.

'Yes,' Rawson agreed, 'but there's still three too many looking after us.'

The bombs zipped into the ocean in pairs, seconds apart, raising mounting plumes of water not unlike mushrooms. Four great gouts to starboard were already falling back seaward when the last pair cut through the ocean's crust close astern. One dropped fifteen yards away, and the other no more than five or six yards off. A sudden mountain of water tore through the vessel's wake and piled up against the stern causing the screws to oscillate and throwing the engineer and a stoker clean off their feet.

Rawson turned the ship to starboard again; moments later the Heinkels attacked them again, from a lower altitude.

'Fire as soon as they're within range!'

The pom-pom gunners waited, their loading numbers hovering by them, ill-at-ease. The bridge vibrated as they opened up. It was good to feel the ship shaking and to know she was hitting back.

Britwell gave a hoarse cry as the port gun found a target in the centre plane's starboard wing. A fire developed; one propeller started to feather. But the bombs were on their way again.

This time the ship was straddled. Two bombs forward of the bows, two to port and two more to starboard.

'She must have a charmed life!' Britwell ejaculated.

Rawson grunted. In the well-deck, the

commandos had their palms clapped over their ears as the reverberating underwater explosions clanged endlessly against the ship's sides.

Mercifully, the Luftwaffe gave up at that stage.

In a matter of minutes the crew was busy throwing empties over the side and restocking the ready-use lockers.

An hour later, the landing craft was heading in for the beach at Pizzo, another small community some five miles up-coat from Bagnare. This landing was in very much more adverse conditions than the earlier one. While still a quarter of a mile offshore, the pill-boxes and land batteries spotted them.

'Wouldn't be surprised if the Heinkels didn't tip them off by radio,' Rawson shouted, as tracer and shells tried to find their range.

'This is going to be tough,' Britwell remarked uneasily. 'If we all rush out through the bow doors they'll mow us down like chaff!'

Rawson agreed. He had the situation well thought out. His pom-pom gunners returned the shore fire, putting in short sharp bursts at each of the four pill-boxes on view. The two officers put their heads together, and came up with a plan calculated to lessen the casualties.

The canvas covers were rolled away, and the commandos down below received a quick briefing. Britwell was their C.O. now, since two officers had been killed in the Bagnare clash, and all others senior to him had been wounded.

His own calmness communicated itself to them. They admired him. They way he had cleared the Bagnare beach would never be forgotten by them. Calmly, and without undue haste, thirty men came up out of the bowels of the ship to crouch along the port rails. Another thirty followed them and took up positions to starboard. Previous to this, the crew had unfurled scrambling nets down either side.

At the first scrape on the bottom, Rawson killed the engines. The bow door crashed open with a mighty splash. Amid countless probing bursts of bright tracer bullets, three-score commandos threw themselves forward and ran for the beach, fanning out as they went.

The parties on the rails went over the sides at the same instant, holding their weapons high. Britwell, himself, called out a hasty farewell, and shinned down a Jacob's Ladder. Rawson started one engine, swinging the craft to port so as to protect the men still sheltering in the well-deck during the few seconds left to them.

A hoarse shout from Britwell, and they surged forward.

'All out, Skipper!' Jones bellowed, from the wheelhouse vantage point.

Rawson closed the bow doors. With both engines in reverse he moved into deep water. Both pom-poms were still firing bursts ashore. He nodded to the loading numbers, who watched him anxiously. Suddenly, he had an idea. It might help.

As the commandos splashed, fell, crawled and crumpled, firing all the time, he reached for his loud-hailer. He blinked at it, switched it on, and filled his mighty lungs to their full capacity.

'Up the commandos!' he yelled, his magnified voice carrying far up the beach. Here and there, an anxious Briton risked a quick glance back, and blinked with sudden pride at the sight he presented. To them it seemed as though his gigantic body was also magnified. He stood there, clenched fist raised. They heard him refill his lungs, and then . . .

'*Blighty forever! See you at Wembley some time!*'

As the craft stood out to sea, Britwell rose to his feet, waved his men forward, and advanced at a double marching pace. Every ten seconds he pulled the pin out of a grenade and tossed it. His aim was good. He had learned it at cricket. One pill-box fell silent. Over on the extreme right, a handful of daring men were getting in close — too close for the defenders' guns to bear.

But there were many khaki-clad forms lying still on the sand.

Rawson pondered this through his glasses. He determined to stay in the area as long as he dare, in case things took a turn for the worse. Ten long minutes dragged by, when the situation ashore was touch and go. The pom-poms were silent now, as the ammunition was running low.

A pimply-faced A.B. pounded Rawson's shoulder. He lowered the glasses and took a signal from the wireless-telegraphist.

'Is that radio still working?' he asked.

The W/T operator frowned. He could never tell when the skipper was joking with him. Rawson's face was serious enough when he looked up from the signal. He peered at the youth as though he did not believe what was written.

It said:

Proceed to rendezvous point ten miles west of Salerno Gulf. All L.C.s to assist in large-scale landings.

He wondered if the commando raid had been really necessary.

9

Scoop Britwell's deliberations about the Allies having to put another sizeable force ashore before Naples could be taken were very much to the point.

As early as September 6th, the main assault convoy of cruisers, destroyers, minesweepers, tank landing ships, troop carriers, L.C.T.s and assault craft was already on its way from the assault port of Tripoli.

General Mark Clark's Fifth Army, which was the assault force, consisted of the British Tenth Corps, and the American Sixth Corps.

The beaches around Salerno Gulf were chosen for the actual assault. The problem of where to land had been carefully assessed. The Salerno beaches were conveniently near to Naples, the immediate objective. Furthermore, they were near enough to Sicily for adequate Allied air cover to be provided. Spitfires based in Sicily, provided they carried extra fuel tanks, could remain over the assault beaches for as long as twenty minutes.

The sea approach was good. The beaches could not have been better. There were snags, however, which were to be thrown into relief later.

Originally, General Clark had wanted to attack north of Naples, but this would have meant that the R.A.F. would be too far from bases to operate effectively.

The actual size of the strike force had had to be cut because of the shortage of landing craft. And two airborne units had to be left behind for special jobs. On paper, General Clark had under his command only three divisions, backed up by two companies of American rangers and two commandos. Not very many more troops, in fact, than had been landed in Calabria to fight across the toe.

The High Command had their headaches. Sixty thousand Germans, for instance, had escaped into Italy across the Straits before the Allies took Messina. The Italians still had 180,000 troops in southern Italy, although it was hoped — in the light of secret negotiations between Marshal Badoglio and General Eisenhower — that they would lay down their arms.

Soldiers and sailors of the strike force heard of the negotiations while still at sea on the 8th.

General Eisenhower made a broadcast at 1800 hours to the effect that the Italians had concluded terms for an armistice. It had been arranged that Marshal Badoglio should broadcast to the Italian people at the same time, telling them of the surrender. But even as he broadcast, the general must have had serious doubts about whether Badoglio would honour his agreement.

If Badoglio had been in full possession of all the facts about the actual numbers of Allied troops in his country, he would certainly have hesitated to go ahead with the armistice, fearful of German strength and superiority. When first he commenced negotiations, the Italian marshal had insisted that fifteen Allied divisions should be landed before he could co-operate. But the Allies only had six, all told. When told that the invasion would take place whether he surrendered or not, he must have agreed, but with reluctance.

Eisenhower's broadcast completely mystified the rank and file of soldiers and sailors in the strike force. For a time, they did not know how the surrender would affect them. Would they be able to walk ashore unmolested, or what? Such ideas were soon to be knocked out of their heads.

Listeners at Allied High Command waited in vain for Badoglio to make his speech to the Italian people. Did this mean that he had gone back on his promise? Would the Salerno force have to fight Italians, as well as Germans?

The strike force drew steadily nearer their objective. Allied High Command was still in a quandary. Finally, one-and-a-quarter hours late, Marshal Badoglio did come on the air and say what was expected of him. The planners must have lost pounds in perspiration.

As soon as the armistice news came

through, warships escorting the Salerno convoys slipped away to take the British Ist Airborne Division to Taranto, in the heel. This was the beginning of another plan to capture the south-eastern area as a prelude to a big push up both coasts. Two forces would be needed for a big advance. This was necessitated by the bulky obstacle down the middle of the country; that awkward geographical location, the Apennine Mountain range.

The airborne division captured Taranto, as planned, late on September 9th. In addition to the town, the nearby airfields were also overrun. Columns at once advanced on Bari and Brindisi, up the Adriatic coast.

★   ★   ★

The main body of the British 10th Corps started the main Salerno assault.

Between midnight and three a.m., the mighty concourse of ships reached the anchorage nine miles offshore. Almost at once, German searchlights started to sweep the foreshore. Orange flames betrayed hasty demolitions in the harbour area. Obviously the enemy were much on the alert.

No previous bombardment by sea or air had given them any clue as to where the assault was to take place. The surprise element, which had been thought to be worthwhile, was negatived at the outset. In spite of Italy's surrender, the Germans were very much on their toes.

At about three-thirty a.m., the first assault boats grounded. Shock troops splashed and fought their way ashore under a curtain of covering fire from destroyers, flak ships and rocket ships. Half-deafened, they threw themselves into the hand-to-hand fighting which was the only method by which the beaches could be won.

The German Panzers who engaged them were not in large numbers, but the defence was cleverly based upon a series of strong-points, from which a heavy fire was poured down upon the invaders. These strong-points were well supported by mobile guns, tanks, and armoured cars.

Right from the start, Salerno was no pushover.

★ ★ ★

As part of the terms of surrender, Marshal Badoglio had agreed to hand over the Italian Grand Fleet, which had for so long been a thorn in the side of Admiral of the Fleet Sir Andrew Cunningham, the C-in-C, Mediterranean.

During the first day of the Salerno assault, Allied reconnaissance aircraft identified the main capital units of the Italian fleet, steaming south, according to plan, from the ports of Genoa and Spezia. On an ordered course they came south by a westerly course round the island of Corsica, so as to avoid interference by the Germans.

Instead of proceeding south, past Sardinia, the Italian Admiral misread his instructions and brought the fleet through the Strait of Bonifacio which separates Sardinia from Corsica. This caused a disaster. The Luftwaffe spotted them, and as a result, the capital ship *Roma* was hit by one of the new German glider-bombs. She blew up and sank causing many unnecessary deaths.

The Grand Fleet, however, did arrive in Malta on the following day, escorted by H.M. Ships *Warspite* and *Valiant*. This was a great triumph for the C-in-C, who must have felt greatly satisfied when he sent off his historic signal to the Admiralty.

★   ★   ★

That first dawn on the beaches of Salerno was a time of terrible revelation. As the early morning greyness changed to white light, the British and American soldiers who had struggled ashore under an endless fusillade of machine-gun and 88mm. fire, first saw the magnitude of the task which lay before them.

Back from the beaches, the plain was no more than a small triangular strip, completely dominated by the nearest peaks of the Apennines. From the Sorrento peninsula they stretched away south to Agropoli. The apex of the triangle, in the valley of the river Sele, was ominously overlooked by the 1,500′ peak, Mount Eboli. Also under its domination were the two small towns of Battipaglia and Eboli, through which ran important roads and the railway.

Progress north, out of the coastal strip around Salerno, could only be achieved one way. That was through two mountain passes strongly held by large forces of the enemy. The plain of Naples, therefore, seemed to be a very remote and distant goal.

Much further south, the Eighth Army, weary from the beginning after the breakneck campaign in Sicily, was slowly and arduously working its way northwards.

Some ten miles north of Bagnare, where the commando had first gone ashore, the spearhead of their columns approached a small village. Ever since Bagnare the Germans had done all in their power to make the roads impassable behind them. As a result, the bulldozers had come to play an increasingly important part.

After his Herculean work on the beaches at Reggio, Dusty Lewis, the bulky pioneer, had been allowed to continue in his self-appointed job of driver to a 'dozer. Accompanied by his buddy, Corporal Harris, he was always to be found well to the fore, tidying up the road on either side.

His enormous physical energy more than made up for any mental slowness. He handled the bulldozer as though he had been born to it, and none of its vagaries in any way unsettled him.

At the outskirts of the village, which appeared to be perfectly quiet and peaceful, the engineers responsible for the clearance of roads, pulled up for a rest and a quick meal. While the others stepped back off the road into the shelter of the trees so as to enjoy a little shade, Lewis and Harris walked forward, their hands full of mixed fruit.

Lewis was impressed with the debris which lay ahead of him. All along the centre of the road were large stones and pebbles from a dry-stone wall which appeared to have been knocked over intentionally.

'Cor, Nipper,' he muttered huskily, 'them Jerries is the most destructive blokes I've ever come acrost.'

Harris cracked a walnut between his teeth. He spat out small pieces of shell, frowning at the wizened nut inside.

'So would you be, me old mate, if you'd a ruddy army right on your tail keepin' you movin' all the time. 'Ow would you like it, always on the move? No time to pull up, and make yourself agreeable to the *signorinas*? It ain't 'uman, if you arsks me. Even a soldier's got feelin's. Come to think of it, I'm gettin' brahned off wiv all this foot-sloggin' meself. I could just do with a nice cushy billet in one o' these villages for the duration. What do you say to that?'

Lewis threw a heap of rind over his shoulder. He spat on his hands and rubbed them together. 'A quiet number? You can count me out, Nipper, boy. This bulldozin' lark's the best thing that ever 'appened to me. Keeps me fit, makes me feel useful. Why, I could go eight rounds right now with anybody, British or Jerry

— wouldn't need to take me shirt off!'

The two of them came to a stop, and looked back the way they had come. Harris rolled an unlighted cigarette round his battered underlip. He eyed his large buddy speculatively.

'Know what, cocker? If they keeps you on this drivin' lark much longer you're goin' to finish the campaign wiv a swelled 'ead!'

Lewis took a playful poke at him. 'That won't worry me none, Nip. Just so long as I don't get to 'ear the bells!'

★ ★ ★

Ten minutes later, the bulldozer was heaving, carving and thrusting its way up the road again. Much of its bright yellow paint had peeled off with the buffeting it had received in the past few days. It was also noisier, but it still worked.

Lewis sat poker-faced at the controls. Five yards up, back out. Turn her round a bit, then push again. Leave the debris tidily by the roadside. Two runs at it, and then he switched over and started

135

pushing it away towards the other side. It broke the monotony, which Lewis at times felt; though he would have denied it.

Half an hour's hard graft brought them almost level with a row of four cottages set back on the seaward side in an acre of olive groves. Harris was taking a ride on the back of the 'dozer, idly dragging his feet and keeping a watchful eye open for Captain Carter who was never far away.

Neither of them glanced at the buildings. They appeared to be uninhabited. When Lewis was not looking down at his rammer, he was looking ahead. And the last time he had looked up, he saw that the road was comparatively clear just past the cottages. Soon he would be able to take a breather. It was good to be able to drift off now and again to do some foraging for grub. Grub had always been his lasting passion.

Right opposite the middle pair of cottages, the 'dozer gave a sudden lurch. Harris, on the back, cracked his head against the metalwork behind him.

''Ere, what the 'ell are you playin' at, Dusty?' he protested in a loud voice.

Lewis gave a deep belly laugh. He said: 'Thought you was asleep, mate!'

Before Harris could reply in his usual salty vein two Spandau machine-guns opened up on the 'dozer from the upper storey of one of the cottages. Harris had spoken his last word. Slowly, his riddled body slid off the back of the machine and folded in the road so recently cleared.

Bullets whipped in all round Lewis, clanging on the metal frame above him, and snapping at his fingers on the controls. He took a deep breath of surprise, opened his throttle and pushed his huge frame back against the shield behind him.

By a miracle, he was unhurt. In a few yards he was clear of the debris. He continued to move forward, his machine weaving precariously from side to side. He had progressed some twenty yards when his somewhat sluggish brain got round to thinking about Harris. He peered back, half out of his seat. More bullets flew at him. He blinked hard as though that would shift them.

Then he saw Harris. His battered face

gradually changed. It grew mottled. His chest began to heave. Harris was dead. He knew it. He began to work up into one of the scarcely sane rages which had laid him open to punishment in the past and so shortened his boxing career.

'My buddy's dead . . . Nipper's dead!' Once he started muttering he went on, speaking his thoughts aloud through clenched teeth. 'What am I doin' drivin' on as if nothin' had happened? I got to go back there an' sort out them Nazis. It's my job to sort 'em out. Nipper's my business. I got to go back there quickly, before Carter an' the others take the job right out of my hands, like they always want to. Like they always want to make out I'm no good, except for punchin' . . . like all them other geysers in civvy street . . . makin' out I'm a no good punchdrunk . . . I am some good . . . I — I'm a 'dozer driver . . . I'm a good 'dozer driver. It takes a strong man to drive this machine. I'm a strong man. I'll drive it right back across Europe, if they give me a chance. But first I got to get them Nazis.

'I know . . . the 'dozer'll do it for me . . . that's a good idea . . . a smart idea . . . the sort of idea Nip would've liked. The 'dozer! That's how I'll do it, with the dozer . . . '

He blinked as a wide wooden gate appeared on the left. The bullets had ceased by now, but he knew the Germans hadn't gone. They were waiting and watching for a chance to take more shots at him. To riddle his body like they had done to Nipper . . . to kill him, so that Lucy wouldn't get to see him any more.

Well, he'd show them . . . He swung the machine sharply to the left, through the gate. Round the back, that was the idea; where they would not expect him. Jutting out from the sidewall of the end cottage was a low wall, running downhill towards the sea. Lewis sized it up quickly. Without slackening speed, he raised his rammer a couple of feet and charged at it. The top of thc wall spilled over ahead of him. The machine rocked through the gap.

The backs of the cottages were screened from him by a lattice-work fence, lush with green creepers and bright flowers. He didn't want to waste any time before he tackled the building. The Nazis might take fright and run away.

Breathing gustily through his broken nose, he turned the machine sharply to the left again. In a matter of seconds he had crashed through the lattice-work and made juddering contact with the rear wall of one of the centre cottages.

A large section, between door and window, gave before him. He crouched as the machine bored on, covered in dust and falling plaster. Faintly he could hear cries of alarm above the engine noise. He ignored them. He knew exactly what he was doing. He braked, backed a yard and turned to the right. A thinner, connecting wall gave way before him this time. Centuries old beams dropped from the disintegrating ceiling like a disturbed skeleton, clattering off the frame and falling in all directions. He charged through another connecting wall, then turned and steam-rollered his way out through a front wall. Four beams had hit him on the head, but he had scarcely

140

blinked. Figures appeared at another door further down, but they retreated indoors again, their faces showing flagrant disbelief.

Down the road, a wary patrol of infantry called to Lewis. They got no reply. He charged another section of the front, buffeted his way through it and turned sharply, demolishing the third connecting wall. He sneezed and coughed, but resolutely carried on with his task. An ominous groaning in the upper storeys had no effect on him. He was knocking out another section at the back when the whole structure started to fall inwards like a pack of cards. Two startled soldiers fell across the machine, cried in pain and fell off it into the mounting debris. Frantically trying to keep out of the way of the machine, they fought and scrabbled about. One of them saw the roof, through the fallen ceiling, just as Lewis was beginning to take a personal interest in him.

The falling started with a mighty creak and rumble. The machine stopped in the middle of it. The crashing went on for nearly five minutes. After that there was only the gentle patter-patter of falling plaster . . .

Lewis was still upright, and in place in the driving seat when the wondering infantry probed the wreckage. Shellfire could not have made a better job of the demolition. Buried in the wreckage were eight German soldiers, all of them past help. Each of them had the same stricken, unbelieving look etched deeply into his face.

At first they thought the big man was dead. He did not answer when they called to him. But after a moment or two, he blinked and sneezed. Two men tried to haul him clear. He thrust them out of the way with a mighty forearm. Presently, he spat out, then climbed out with no more concern than if he was on an open beach.

He walked out at the back, and stood, hands in pockets, blinking in the sunlight, remote and withdrawn.

One of the infantrymen shook his head. 'This lot's a bit beyond me, townie,' he said with feeling, 'but there's one thing I do know for sure. There's no power on earth'll ever dislodge this bulldozer again.'

'Spoken like a true prophet, chum. They'll probably find it in a thousand years' time, buried under a few tons of lava from Vesuvius,' the other opined.

Lewis had heard their words. He turned round, looking from one to the other. Then, blinking slowly, he removed his tin hat and gazed at the buried machine, as though he were seeing a memorial tablet in a cemetery. The others silently watched him, guessing at his secret thoughts.

10

Although almost completely surrounded by land on all sides the sunny Mediterranean has its ugly side; particularly in the western half, it is often subjected to very sudden and violent winds. The most dreaded one which blows across from the south of France towards the coast of Italy is called the mistral. All seasoned seamen have reason to fear it.

The mistral which sprang up on the second night of the Salerno affair had far-reaching repercussions.

It made itself felt in the offices of the joint Allied High Command, many hundreds of miles away in Algiers. All through that first day, although the Allies were supposed to have air superiority — as regards numbers — the Luftwaffe had made itself a grave nuisance in the Gulf.

And then, in the last few hours of daylight, the mistral sprang into being. It swept out of the north-west, rocking the ships at anchor, and filling the men lying out in the open ashore with a dread foreboding.

The vital landing craft were the ships which suffered most of all. Three of them which were inshore, disgorging ammunition and stores, found that they could not pull clear of the beach.

One or two wily skippers whose boats had taken a pounding on a similar occasion during the invasion of Sicily craftily kept on going out to sea. They knew the hazards. It was better to be missing for a trip or two than to end up as a battered hulk on the shore, no longer fit for anything.

Rawson's boat was alongside a large American landing ship. For two hours his men had been stacking crates in the well-deck as fast as they were slung out of the mother ship on the cranes.

In spite of tyres lashed to the guardrails to act as fenders, the large and small vessels began to grind together. The crew began to mutter among themselves. From time to time they glanced up at the bridge where Rawson sprawled wearily in his canvas chair.

He found his wits slow to adjust to the new and threatening situation. Since the repair job in Messina, he had never napped for more than two hours together. The strain was beginning to tell.

This load they had just taken on board was largely ammunition. That presented a problem in itself. With the mounting waves it would become increasingly more difficult to keep it dry. He weighed up the chances of doing a quick trip inshore. He could make it, he thought. But would he be able to get off again?

He knew what would happen if he was caught on the shore. He had seen it happen to many of his fellow L.C. skippers. The waves would pound the craft higher and higher; none of the anchors provided for these craft could hold them in these conditions. Once high on the beach, her screws would be damaged. The propeller shafts would take a beating.

After that, they could be written off. They would be no further use to the war effort — not even as a static water tank!

Rawson heaved himself to his feet. The atmosphere was becoming oppressive, and the whining wind made conversation difficult. He reached for the loud-hailer.

'A-hoy, there! Can you hear me, Captain?'

He pointed the hailer at the landing ship's bridge. An anxious face under a laurel-peaked cap appeared over the bridge sponsons and peered down at him.

'Sure, I can hear you, Skip! How're you makin' out?'

'Not too well! The guardrail's taking a bit of a beating! I think we ought to push off shortly, before you do us some real damage!

'That's surely up to you, Skip. You got your ship to consider, an' you know these waters better'n I do. I'd say the beach don't look too healthy from up here! One or two of your L.C. boys appear to be in trouble already!'

The crew had stopped packing and were standing up, listening to the shouted conversation. 'Well, there's one thing,' put in a seaman, 'this little blow-up 'll keep the Luftwaffe off our backs for a while.'

'Shut up!' Petty Officer Jones barked sharply.

Rawson heard him. He winked down at the sweating working party. He called up to the big ship once more.

'You've made up my mind for me, Captain! I'm pulling out straight away. I'm going to give the beach a wide berth, though, till the mistral blows out!'

'O-kay, o-kay, now,' drifted back the easy rejoinder, 'just take it easy, now. You'll be back . . . '

Rawson dropped the loud-hailer back on its hook. He stretched and yawned loudly. Then, leaning over the windbreak, he grinned tiredly down at the working party.

'All right, Swain, have everything lashed down as soon as you can! We're holding onto that little lot till things quieten down a bit. Send Scotty up to the galley. We could do with a brew up all round. And a sandwich, as well. Better send up another hand to help him. I'm hungry!'

Five minutes later, Petty Officer Jones

clumped back into the wheelhouse, tired and ill-humoured. He slung his duffle-coat round his shoulders rather carelessly. He was doing up the toggles when he found he had knocked down a tiny battered pin-up of his little blonde wife.

He bent down and retrieved her from the deck.

'Stap me, Mew, what wouldn't I give to be curled up in bed under your mother's eiderdown with you . . . ' he muttered fiercely to her . . . 'instead of getting ready for another infernal little Mediterranean mystery trip with no sleep and a couple of hundred thousand projies for company!'

He was so angry that when he pinned her up again, the drawing pin went through her forehead.

★   ★   ★

Some of the crew were still eating their snack at their stations when Rawson started to move the boat.

In a hostile wind and buffeting sea he knew just how awkward a flat-bottomed

149

square-bowed craft could be. During his first command, some eighteen months earlier, a contrary wind had blown up in the Firth of Clyde. After being instructed to go alongside the Flotilla Leader, port side to, by a somewhat unfeeling F.O., he had tried for half an hour to bring her bows round without success.

After giving it up, he had been forced to tie up starboard side to. To make matters worse he had carried away part of the Flotilla Leader's guardrail. The Flotilla Officer had held it against him for nearly a year, till in similar circumstances the positions were reversed.

The Flotilla Officer had made a worse botch of the job than he had. After that, they had become bosom friends.

Loaded with the ammunition and stores, L.C.T. 17 was facing inshore. He knew he had to turn her while still getting some protection from the wind in the lee of the larger vessel. He worked out his plan for turning her most carefully. The stern cables were cast loose first. As the stern started to swing away, he went slow astern on the port engine. This accelerated the parting.

Just at the right moment he had the forward moorings cast off.

Cutting the port engine, he bellowed down to the wheel-house. 'Hard a-port, Swain!'

Jones threw tea-leaves in a wide arc over the side and complied.

'Half ahead, both!' He shouted the order down the engine-room voice-pipe in addition to working the telegraph. If there was any delay it could be very hazardous. The edge of the beach was a white line of spume by now.

The engines rumbled into life. As the plates vibrated beneath his feet, Rawson breathed a deep sigh of relief. So far, so good. The bow started to come round too quickly.

'Starboard, thirty, Swain!'

Jones made the adjustment. The bows straightened. Two minutes later, they were clear of the shelter afforded by the larger vessel. A heavy great green mountain of water punished the bows, making the craft shudder from stem to stern. Aluminium cups and pans clattered across the galley to the accompaniment of

Able Seaman Scott's cursing tongue.

'Straighten her up, Swain!'

The wheel spun and still the great head of water pushed the bows steadily round to port.

'Hard a-starboard, give it everything!'

Rawson, Jones and half a dozen other men in exposed places shared the tension as they waited to see if the craft would answer. Reluctantly, and with much uncalled-for slewing, she came slowly round to face the bow sea.

The tension eased a little. Slowly, the craft fought its way a mile clear of the anchorage. Rawson kept her there with just enough revs to counteract the power of the relentless waves.

An hour past. It dragged into two, and then three. The crew changed watches, but Rawson and Jones were still there, holding on. They drank scalding hot ship's cocoa which afforded them some small comfort. Dodd was napping on his telegraph platform down below, too far gone to keep awake. The smell of crude oil had finally fixed him.

At two a.m., the mistral started to blow

itself out. There was a slow easing in the motion of the sea. Rawson felt it as he lay slumped in his canvas chair. He muttered to himself.

'Swain,' he called, 'let's get to hell out of here. We're going to drop anchor. The boys are too far gone to unload this lot for a while.'

The three key men made the adjustments to bring the ship about. It answered easily. About half a mile offshore the stern anchor was let go. It held. Apart from two lookouts the craft became a metal dormitory.

An hour after dawn, the heroes of L.C.T. 17 landed their load of materials. They drew off and without awaiting instructions, they went to the assistance of the seven L.C.T.s piled up on the beach. Two of them had been hauled off when the enemy came to life and started to make his presence felt.

The beach-head was unbelievably narrow. Systematically, the guns on the hills in the background started to pound it. It was as well the Fifth Army was suitably dug in. Overhead the Luftwaffe and the Allied

Strategic Air Command started a day of endless dogfights in an effort to assist their respective ground forces.

High on the list of casualities for the previous day were the bulldozer drivers. Six American drivers had been killed while working their machines. This had left the American beach sector unbelievably cluttered. It also had some bearing on an urgent signal which Rawson received from the cruiser flagship. It said:

S.O. to L.C.T. 17. Proceed at once to Pizzo. Embark commando and bulldozer drivers if possible. Return immediately to Red Beach.

Joyce, Rawson's Southampton-born signalman, winked an acknowledgement with his Aldis lamp.

'There's one thing about this ship, Skip,' he remarked, 'she certainly gets in plenty of sea-time!'

'How true,' the skipper muttered, 'a few months swinging round the buoy at Scapa won't come amiss after this Italian lark. Just think of it, watch ashore every afternoon, and nothing to do but drink beer in the canteen at Flotta. Fair makes you thirsty to think of it!'

His face clouded over as they headed south. He was beginning to wonder if the High-Ups hadn't made a blunder or two lately. This commando at Pizzo, for instance. Unless he was mistaken, they were about to collect the same bunch they'd put ashore not so long ago. From the pasting the Home Counties Commando was getting when they left there might conceivably be very few survivors to make the trip!

He began to assess young Britwell's chances of survival. After all, officers had no very great expectation of life in wartime. The snipers sorted out the men with the pips automatically. If the officers were killed the men were disorganised.

For a confirmed optimist, he reflected, he'd been thinking some pretty morbid thoughts just lately.

11

Leutnant Strauss, the commanding officer of the small Hermann Goering detachment which had captured Scoop Britwell, had no intention of being cut off by the twin Allied fork moving up the toe of Italy.

In the first four days after Scoop had been apprehended, they covered eighty miles, keeping always to mountain tracks, and maintaining a sharp lookout for signs of Allied encroachment.

Early on the fifth day a small town called Cosenza was approached with great caution; it was the first settlement which Britwell had set eyes on since San Giovanni. As soon as the Germans' grey uniforms were seen, the town went absolutely dead.

Britwell peered about him, wondering if there was any special motive for trekking there. He was to find out quite soon. Cosenza was the end of a railway line.

Strauss led his detachment onto the

railway platform. Like everywhere else, there were no people about. But there was a small locomotive, and behind it, two carriages of inferior design, with wooden seats.

Strauss debated with *Feldwebel* Ludecke about their find.

'The driver and fireman probably live in the village,' the be-spectacled N.C.O. suggested. His somewhat prominent eyes glinted as he added: 'I'm sure we could persuade the population to give us some help in the matter. Not much pressure would be needed.'

Strauss grunted. He knew what the N.C.O. meant. Given half a chance, he would be in the cottages, beating up the old folk and raping the women. He wanted to get among them and act the all-conquering soldier. Looking for the engine-driver would just be an excuse.

'I don't think we've got time,' he answered shortly. 'The British must have landed in the east by now. Any delay might still result in our being cut off.'

'Then what do you suggest, *Herr Leutnant*?' Ludecke asked meekly. He was shrewd enough to know what the officer thought of him and he intended to keep his nose clean. Strauss wouldn't always be with them. One of these days the enemy might bump him off.

★   ★   ★

Britwell tried hard to overhear their conversation. He was as interested as any of the others to know what their future movements were likely to be. But they were talking in whispers, so he gave it up.

Since his capture, the *Leutnant* had seen to it that he was treated decently. At the end of the first day's forced march, he had been interrogated for over an hour by the officer. He answered easily, but only mentioned things which must be obvious already.

He didn't know how many Allied troops were in Italy or whether the High Command had any particular objectives in southern Italy. Asked about himself, he had told what his own job was.

Strauss, quite surprisingly, had heard of the *Daily Globe*. In fact he had spent six months in England, learning the language in 1937. Although there was no particular sign of sympathy in him, Britwell thought that he had no hatred for the British. Perhaps, like so many other educated Germans, he merely felt it a pity that the Germans and the British were not fighting side by side.

A sharp command brought the party to attention. Ludecke addressed them. He asked for two volunteers to drive and stoke the locomotive. At first nobody stepped forward.

'If we don't clear out of here quickly,' Strauss put in quietly, 'we may soon be apprehended by the British and made prisoners.'

Three men then stepped forward, and the services of two of them were accepted. While the boiler was heated with coal and wood, another party of four slipped away to do some foraging. They were warned to keep away from the local population.

Half an hour later, the tiny train was rolling eastward at a good thirty-five miles an hour.

Britwell had a seat in the rear carriage,

flanked on either side by alert guards. Opposite him, facing the way they were going, Strauss and Ludecke, each nodding in a corner. The motion of the train had a soporific effect on men who had been marching hard, up hill and down dale, for two whole days. Further forward in the train, three or four guttural voices joined together in singing the German version of *Lily Marlene*, but they did not keep it up for long.

Within half an hour the whole party was somnambulent. Olive groves, vineyards and tomato plantations slipped by unnoticed.

The train sped on for perhaps thirty miles up a river valley, veering slightly east of north. By mid-morning they came out on the coastal strip overlooking the wide Gulf of Taranto. Another thirty miles on, they started to cross bridges over three small rivers which found their outlet in the Gulf.

Shortly after midday, the stand-in driver brought the train to a halt at a junction with another line going north-west, up-country. Strauss got out and went forward to talk with him.

Ludecke waited in his corner, hands in pockets, puffing away at a thin German army cigarette. Britwell stared at him. He had not forgotten the way in which he had ratted on him to the soldier, Wilhelm, whose surname he had discovered to be Deutsche.

'A pity we haven't got time to do a little fishing while we're so close to the Gulf,' he suggested half-humorously.

Ludecke glowered at him. He replied with an oath and a torrent of abuse which set the guards sniggering.

Strauss returned quickly; the train made the turn and headed north-west. This, Britwell thought, was definitely more interesting.

★   ★   ★

Two hours later, when the train again, came to a standstill — this time rather more suddenly — Britwell was roused out of a deep sleep. Above the sound of escaping steam, the driver shouted out in alarm.

There was a general scramble for weapons, but before the troops could find out what was wrong, machine-gun bullets started to stream through the open windows. Everyone ducked, as they ricochetted off the walls and ceiling and flew in all directions.

'*Englanders!*' a hoarse voice called from the passage.

From his unbecoming position on the floor with Ludecke's boots too close to his face for comfort, Britwell's spirits started to rise. One of the guards collapsed with a bullet in his chest. Following an urgent order from Strauss, the other guard sneaked a quick look to the left — the opposite way from which the initial burst had come. For his pains he fell back with a bullet through his forehead like a third and central eye.

The next compartment erupted as a grenade went off. Britwell began to sweat. If they lobbed another grenade into his compartment, he would die like the rest. What a way to go out . . . Another bullet creased *Leutnant* Strauss' left temple. He collapsed with the merest groan.

'Do something, Ludecke,' bellowed Britwell. 'They're throwing grenades, damn you! We'll all be wiped out in five minutes!'

Ludecke turned to him, his swarthy face dripping perspiration in his uncertainty. Further forward the spasmodic retaliatory fire grew more intermittent. A cry in English sounded very near, but was indistinguishable.

Muttering to himself, Ludecke came to his knees, a dirty kerchief in his hand. He knotted it on his rifle with shaky fingers and slowly raised it into view on the left side.

'Tell them to stop firing, you stupid bastard!'

Ludecke's voice failed him the first time, but fear is a great prompter. He tried again. His voice rose almost to a shriek, and the firing from the train stopped.

Britwell rolled to his knees in a short lull.

'Hold your fire out there!' he bellowed in his strongest voice. He heard a voice say. 'Hold it' and he knew that they now had a chance.

He shouted again: 'The officer's right

aft, here, wounded. Senior N.C.O is with him!'

Cautious footsteps approached the rear compartment.

'All right, nobody'll jump you. You can stick your head in if you want!'

'I hope you know what you're talking about, chum,' a voice said just below the window on the right.

'So do I,' returned Britwell cheerfully. 'Hurry it up, though, the suspense is killing me.'

A frowning bronzed face with a blue-stubble chin suddenly appeared framed in the window. Only the face showed in a green helmet and cowl. The business end of a Sten pushed its way over the sill. The grimace took in the scene and slowly relaxed.

'Don't tell me, I'll guess,' Britwell said brightly. 'No, it's not the Arabian Nights, it's the perishing hostile paratroops. I'm Scoop Britwell. Glad to meet you.'

The face nodded and the Sten pointed at Ludecke.

'Order your men out on the line, this side!'

'Go on then,' Britwell added, 'you heard him.'

Ludecke rose slowly, hands aloft; he stepped out into the corridor and gave the necessary order. The doors were opened cautiously and the cowed Germans dropped to the line, one at a time. Weapons clattered on the permanent way.

Britwell moved out after them. Behind him Strauss was groaning, but he had not regained consciousness. The newspaperman found himself among two-score of grim-looking paratroops in green smocks and head-dresses. Some of them were still wearing red berets.

He stepped to one side, and offered his hand to the officer with the blue chin. He was completely at his ease now.

'Captain Mason, 2nd Airborne Brigade, up from Taranto,' he said. He glanced at Britwell's shoulder flashes and his face broke into a mischievous grin. 'Great Scot, you war correspondents go to great lengths to get your material don't you? I've never heard of you being attached to the German Army before, though.'

The paratroopers searched the train thoroughly and without undue haste; the wounded and a few dead were brought out of it. Strauss walked out under his own steam. He gave Britwell a rueful smile, and then moved off, after his own men.

Britwell watched him go. He was saying: 'You know, Captain, that sense of humour will be the death of you someday. All the same, I was never more pleased to see the British army.'

They went on chatting for a few more minutes. Britwell saw the tree across the line which had brought about the halt. He learned that they were half a mile outside the town of Potenza, sixty miles due east of the Salerno beaches. The big seaborne landing had been made in the early hours of that morning.

Britwell went along to the paratroops' bivouac and ate a hearty meal while the captain brought him up to date on the latest war situation.

A narrow fringe of trees separated the railway line from a road on the east side of the place where the paratroops had ambushed the train. One solitary person had observed the one-sided encounter. She was Marisa Perucci, a tall slim Italian girl of twenty-two years. Her high-cheekbones, intelligent dark green eyes and general carriage marked her as something above the average run of Italian peasants. Her long black hair was caught back in a comb at the nape of her neck. Her off-the-shoulder green summer frock, and ear-rings of a darker shade showed her good taste.

On this occasion she had a dark shawl modestly covering her shapely shoulders and masking the plunging line of her pleasing bosom. Rope-soled sandals completed her visible clothing, and she carried in her hand a canvas shopping bag.

As the Germans were marched away, she sat down with a sigh and ate some fruit. If war taught one anything, it was patience.

She came to her feet again as the khaki-clad Englishman reappeared with the officer. They shook hands and the stranger walked through the trees towards her, shouting a cheery farewell over his shoulder.

Necessity made her bold. She stepped out from behind a tree, in front of him.

'*Signore*, please. I would not trouble you ordinarily, but could you tell me, will the soldiers allow the train to go on to Battipaglia?'

Britwell eyed her with interest. Her perfect English came as a surprise. He saw that she had something akin to fear behind her eyes. When he had removed the masking sun-glasses, he smiled easily.

'Strange you should ask that, *signorina*. I asked the question myself. The answer is no. The paratroop officer will not permit it — at least not for several days. Battipaglia, I understand, is still in the hands of the Germans. Do you have to go there?'

She gave him a fleeting smile. 'Yes, you may not think my business terribly important. I am — was, that is — a school-teacher in Battipaglia. My school was bombed and my father sent me to stay with my aunt, here in Potenza. Since then Battipaglia has been bombed several times. My father is quite old. I feel he will need me. The difficulty is how to get there.'

The two of them had stepped clear of the trees and were walking slowly up the road towards the town.

'I take it you would not wish to make the journey alone?' Britwell said thoughtfully.

A small pink tongue traced the line of her full lips. She smiled again. 'You are very shrewd, *signore*. I am afraid. The Germans, well, they are not so gentle with women as the British are.'

'All kinds of men wear the British uniform, *signorina*. But enough of that. I do not want to put you off. My duty takes me in the direction of Battipaglia. Perhaps we could travel together?'

To his surprise, she agreed without hesitation.

'With you I would feel safe, *signore* — if you are sure I would not be in the way?'

With only the slightest hesitation, she stepped closer and slipped her free hand into his. Britwell was touched by her trust. He took her bag and carried it.

'I shall be glad of your company. You can guide me,' he said. 'But tell me, do you always trust strange men so readily?'

Marisa chuckled. 'No, of course not. Say, in your case, it is a woman's intuition. I think you are a gentleman. You take no joy in seeing war. From what I observed, you were a prisoner of the Germans, and yet, when you were freed and they were captured, you took no revenge on them.'

Britwell smiled broadly. For hours in the train, he had planned what he would do to get even with Wilhelm and the treacherous Ludecke. Wilhelm, he planned to thrash, and Ludecke, the snake, was to have the lenses pushed out of his spectacles. It was just that when the opportunity presented itself for revenge, he couldn't be bothered. He was too interested in eating, and talking to the captain.

He explained this to her, and she said that it proved he was not really a vengeful man. Presently they entered the town. Marisa's aunt greeted Britwell warmly. It was not difficult to persuade him to spend the night at her house. After the arduous march with the Germans he needed the rest.

A little after daybreak the next day, they set off along the road west. The aunt had provided them with food for the journey. Her last words were a warning to get off the road if they encountered the Germans.

A squadron of Messerschmitts passed overhead soon after they started. They were headed for Salerno, and provided an additional reminder to be wary.

At midday they picnicked in the shade of some olive trees, making a good meal of sandwiches, fruit and wine. Marisa insisted on a short siesta before they went on again. She dropped off into an easy slumber with her head resting lightly on his pack.

He sat with his back to another tree, smoking and watching her, studying the serenity in her face, and marvelling at her trust in him. She had made a great impression in a short time.

During the course of their walking, he had learned that her brother, Lorenzo, had died in jail where he had been placed as an anti-Fascist. As a direct result, her mother had died of a broken heart. It was a sad story which made him want to help all the more. Now she had only her aged father in Battipaglia. If he had survived the bombing. Britwell studied his watch. He shook her gently, assisted her to her feet, and they set off again.

Nearing the German-occupied town, towards teatime, he slackened his pace, not wanting to be parted from her. Marisa sensed this. Without looking at him, she walked a little closer, taking strength from his rugged frame.

Allied bombers revealed the exact location of the town ahead. Through his glasses, he could see a German check-point about a mile ahead. They stopped, looked long at each other, and stepped off the road into an orchard to say their farewells.

With her back slumped against a wall, she looked up into his eyes. 'It was good of you to bring me, Scoop. When the fighting is over in this area, there will always be a welcome for you in my father's house. Everyone knows us, the Peruccis. An old ex-mayor, and a young ex-schoolteacher.'

He took her hands in his. 'Thank you, Marisa. Yes, if at all possible, I will come.' He held up her hands to examine them closer. Again with a woman's intuition, Marisa knew he was interested in her ringless fingers. She took her hands from him, reached up and pulled his head down towards her. Their lips met in the most satisfying kiss Britwell had ever known. When their heads came apart, he saw something new in her eyes. Something he had never seen in the eyes of a woman before. He thought it was a very rare thing, a thing he might never find in his life again.

He said: 'Assuredly I will come to you, Marisa.'

She murmured: '*Cara mia!*'

They kissed again and remained in a close embrace for many minutes. Finally, by mutual consent they parted slowly. Britwell took her by hand into the road again. He gazed up it, as though weighing the hazards she might have to face alone.

Her smile radiated confidence as she brushed his lips with hers once more. Then she was off, swinging the shopping bag and humming an old Neapolitan love song to herself. For the first time, Britwell heard the song of birds which had been there all the time. It was as if he had come alive for the first time. He marvelled at it.

'I will be waiting, *cara mia*!' she promised.

'I'll find you, never fear!'

He stood like a statue, not moving until her distant silhouette waved to him for the last time. One minute more he waited, and then he crossed the road, climbed a wall and set off across country to avoid the alien town.

12

Following the death of Nipper Harris and the loss of his bulldozer, Dusty Lewis was a changed man. Physically he was as good as ever, having escaped from the wrecked buildings with little more than a few bruises and contusions, which to an old battler amounted to nothing.

When Nipper was about, he had chattered to him incessantly, but now he spoke to nobody. Captain Carter, who could get no word out of him, left him very much to his own devices. Then one day, a kindly pioneer had mentioned that there would be more bulldozers on the beach at Salerno.

He said it only in an effort to cheer Lewis, but he could have no idea of the far-reaching effects of his words. The following morning at reveille, Lewis was missing. He had wandered off in the night, obsessed with the idea of finding more bulldozers.

Mile after mile up the coast road he walked, stopping occasionally to rest, and fill his pockets and his stomach with fruit from the plantations. Twenty-four hours after his disappearance he reached Pizzo, where the last assault by the Home Counties 3rd Commando had taken place.

The town had been quiet for twelve hours when he arrived. There was the silence of death around it. Over ninety commandos had died in the fighting, and the survivors had only recently finished burying them. The Germans, who had amounted to twice their number dead, were piled into a communal slit grave with less ceremony.

Sergeant Marsh, on a tour of inspection round the tiny force's perimeter, was the first to see Lewis near a road barrier. Dipper eyed him curiously, thinking at once that the battered face looked familiar. After years as a detective constable, Marsh had a formidable mental picture gallery.

Lewis came to a stop by the barrier, thrust his hands in his pockets, glanced over the men there and then inspected the beach.

'Here, I think I know you, chum,' Dipper exclaimed. 'Aren't you Dusty Lewis, the heavyweight boxer?'

Lewis sniffed noisily through his shattered nose. 'Yes, I been in the fight game. You been in it, too?'

'Not me, chum, I'm just an ex-copper, but I've seen you fight a time or two. You'll 'ave given it up now, I suppose?'

Lewis nodded. He showed no enthusiasm to carry on the conversation, but he allowed Marsh to bring him through the barrier and lead him to the nearest pill-box.

There, Lewis rapidly drank half a bottle of wine. With much prompting, he explained in little more than monosyllables how Nipper Harris had died, and how he had lost his job on the bulldozer.

'Somebody told me there was more bulldozers up 'ere. I suppose you 'aven't got any on this beach, 'ave you?'

'No mate, there's none here, but they'll be using them further north, at Salerno, I shouldn't wonder.'

'I'll 'ave to go there then,' Lewis said shortly.

But the wine and his long walk were having their effect on him. In a few minutes he had fallen asleep with his misshapen head resting on the table. Marsh moved out quietly and advised the other men there not to disturb him.

* * *

Half an hour later, Signalman Joyce's trigger finger was working the Aldis lamp on L.C.T. 17's bridge, half a mile offshore. As he sent the message, his jaws were working rhythmically on a piece of chewing gum, the last out of his tin of action rations.

From a point wide of the pill-boxes up the beach, Tufty Britwell's signaller acknowledged. The grim-faced commando captain dictated his reply. Rawson, an accomplished signaller himself, read the flashed message through his binoculars.

It said: 'Glad to see you again. Party now only ninety strong. Will be ready to embark in thirty minutes. Everything quiet here.'

'Ninety strong?' Rawson murmured. 'That means they took the father and mother of a pasting on that last assault. It's a wonder there's anyone left alive to pick up.'

All this time, Lofty Rawson had never set foot on Italian soil. Although it was not his practice to leave the ship, he decided to make an exception on this occasion. Fifteen minutes later, he walked ashore in thigh-length seaboots, his eyes questing for signs of the recent action.

Marsh came down to meet him. They shook hands.

'Well, Sergeant, it seems as though you've been having a tough time!' Rawson said thoughtfully.

Marsh grimaced. He explained about the arduous business of burying over a hundred of their friends. 'Believe it or not, old Tufty's the only surviving officer. And he didn't get a scratch. In fact, although he doesn't say anything, I've got a feeling he's got some sort of guilt complex about it. Thinks he should have had a few scars, at least.'

Rawson passed over a cigarette. 'Must be a hell of a responsibility taking charge of a couple of hundred blokes you know well. I think it would get me down,' he confessed. 'My job's different. I've only got thirteen to account for all told. And the perishing crate, of course.'

Britwell hurried down to meet them. As he approached Rawson could see that his bronzed face had developed worry lines round the eyes and mouth where they had never been before. They greeted each other warmly and discussed the details for embarkation.

Presently, Rawson pulled off his peaked cap. He scratched his head, where the hair had thinned. 'I don't suppose you chaps know where I could find a bulldozer driver at short notice? It seems a lot of them have been bumped off on the Salerno beaches.'

Dipper Marsh's wide mouth bisected his face in a sudden grin. 'Don't know about drivers,' he said, 'but there's one bloke walked in on us a short while ago who claims to be a driver. Rather an unusual chap — in fact I know him. He's Dusty Lewis, the old heavyweight boxer.'

'That sounds useful,' Rawson replied. He grew thoughtful. 'There was an old pug pushed the L.C. off the beach at Reggio. Couldn't be the same chap, I suppose?'

Right on cue, Lewis emerged from the box where he had been sleeping, blinking his slitted eyes against the bright sun and sniffing the sea-breeze appreciatively.

'That's him,' Rawson cried. 'The lad's a genius with a machine. We'll take him along, if he'll come!'

Lewis had already started down the beach to the ship.

★   ★   ★

It was dawn when Rawson's boat appeared again off Red Beach at Salerno. The sea had given the commandos an easy passage. They lost no time in slipping ashore and reinforcing the weary Americans in their slit trenches.

Lewis, as remote as ever, immediately walked away towards a large bulldozer bedded down under a large camouflage net trimmed with sprigs of tree branches. Watchful Germans fired a quick burst at him from a pill-box a furlong away. Lewis paid no attention. He slipped under the net and stood there, fingering his stubbly chin. This was some machine. It was half as big again as the one he had served his apprenticeship on. The sight of it bucked him up like nothing else could.

A stocky grey-haired American engineer officer in steel-rimmed spectacles had observed Lewis's approach. He ducked under the net and stood beside him.

'Say, you wouldn't be a cat driver, by any chance?' he asked hopefully.

Lewis glanced at him. He said: 'Yer, I'm a driver. Been drivin' one down the coast, till it got fouled up. Wasn't as big as this one, though.'

The American was a director of a firm which made the machines. He began to describe enthusiastically.

'Of course, this cat isn't one of the biggest. It's an eighteen-tonner. But it does a good job. About 300 horsepower.

I'd say it will shift a few tons of earth without straining.'

He went on to explain that there was no normal gearbox. The drive was made through two separate clutches, one for each caterpillar track, which could be engaged or slipped through the two track levers.

He concluded: 'I'd be mighty pleased if you could get this cat working. You'd do a great job. But it's no use making a move until the infantry boys clear those pill-boxes back there. They're just shooting up everything we put against them.' He grinned, patted Lewis on the arm, and reluctantly moved away. 'I'll maybe see you when it gets healthier round here.'

Lewis cracked a fistful of walnuts and crammed the nuts into his mouth. He climbed up on the frame over the driver's seat and took a long look up the beach. Pill-boxes, eh? Well he'd seen a lot of pill-boxes since he first came ashore in Italy. His eyes gleamed. He had an idea. Still munching the nuts, he stripped back the camouflage net. He started up the machine and felt it throb with power. All his confidence in himself returned. He let in the clutches and roared along the beach behind the foremost American trench.

Tired G.I.s stopped shooting and stared at him. Some faces showed puzzlement. Lewis paid them no attention. He rounded the end of the trench and turned inland, heading for a clump of trees, wide of the pill-boxes. He was watchful now, not knowing if the Germans were thick in the road area in the rear.

No fresh guns opened up on him. He ploughed straight into the trees with his rammer — or scraper, as the Americans called it — held low. His first charge bit half through a tree bole. He reversed, attacked it again, and sighed with satisfaction as the tree clattered off the steel frame above him and fell to one side. In five minutes he was through the trees and turning towards the nearest box.

Grinning hugely, he approached it on its blind side. Ten yards away, he put down the scraper and rolled forward a huge heap of earth. This he pushed firmly against the door of the box, effectively trapping the sharpshooters inside. On his next approach he handled the controls delicately. A huge scoopful of earth was carefully manhandled against the nearest gun-slit. Had he not been singing the *Lambeth Walk* to himself he could have heard the German gunners cursing him heartily. He tipped the earth in the slit, and retreated to repeat the operation.

Nearer the sea, the Americans were agog with excitement. The engineer officer who had talked with him had the glasses on him. He shouted instructions into the nearest trench. Joyfully, the Yanks peppered the gunslits with heavy machine-guns. When Lewis moved in again they held their fire.

In a matter of minutes, the slits on one side had been filled in. Lewis moved his cat round the far side, always keeping to the rear. He repeated the same operation on the slits round the other side. No more fire came from within. For good measure he piled a few tons of earth up in front of the slits, just to make sure they could not dig themselves embrasures again.

A roar of North American voices greeted Dusty's accomplishment. But he did not pause in his labours. He moved further north towards the next pill-box. Behind him, 88mm. gunners on the heights to the rear of the beach, had been informed of what was happening. They threw down a curtain of shellfire in front of the immobilised box, which had the effect of turning back a premature rush by G.I.s who had been pinned down for too long.

Lewis, still untouched, filled in the second box, if anything, in less time. As the first shells started to fall near, he pulled out, headed back down the beach, came to a stop and looked back to study his handiwork.

The Americans swarmed round him, pumping his hands and offering him small luxuries out of their packs. He had certainly boosted their morale, even if he had not made it possible for them to make a swift advance.

★   ★   ★

At dusk, after countless short sharp air raids had failed to knock out the 'dozer, he went into action again. Working with precision, he started to prepare new trenches, one hundred yards further forward than the old ones.

Completely wrapped up in his task, he worked to within an hour of dawn. When first light pushed the shadows off the beach, the Americans had occupied the positions he had created for them. Then, and only then, did Lewis finally break off. He stumbled down into a trench, ate a huge meal, washed down with 'shots' out of various flasks, and fell fast asleep. The dawn air attacks made no impression on him whatever.

13

The place where Lewis had done his sterling work with the new bulldozer was some two miles further north than the beach defence-line where the commandos had been put ashore.

Unknown to Britwell's men, when they landed, the situation south of Salerno was becoming critical. Between the British and the American sectors ashore, there was a ten-mile gap. Ever since the initial landings on September 9th, the Germans — well situated on the high ground around the 1500′ peak, Mount Eboli — had been studying the Allied disposition of troops.

Inevitably they had discovered the gap.

Its discovery came at a time when the 60,000 German Panzer troops, which had escaped from Sicily, were ready to go back into the fighting line. And the line of their counter-attack was towards the afore-mentioned gap.

Not lacking in materials, but short in numbers the British and Americans found it increasingly hard to hold them. Gradually the Panzers worked their way closer to the beach.

Lacking numerically the Allies sent urgent communications to the naval forces supporting them some miles out in the Gulf. The navies made a shoot of sorts, but they were considerably handicapped by bad visibility. Due to the incessant movements of military vehicles on wheels and caterpillar tracks, a great pall of yellow dust composed of grit and powdered earth hung over the scene of the operations. To some extent, it rendered negative the attempts of the naval gunners.

★　★　★

This situation left the survivors of the 3rd Home Counties Commando in a pessimistic mood. Three times they had been put ashore, counting this last effort at Salerno. But on each of their other assaults, they had been able to fight their way forward, although they had sustained losses.

Salerno was much different. They were no longer élite spearhead troops with a definite target in view. They were reduced to stop-gap infantrymen, with no hopes of getting to grips personally with the enemy for days.

Most of them were suffering from combat fatigue.

Tufty Britwell knew this, but there was little he could do to brighten his men. His responsibility weighed on his shoulders heavily.

'Ever think about the old days, Tufty?' Marsh remarked, during a lull that afternoon.

'What about them?' Britwell asked with a tired smile.

'Oh, you know, knocking around in the Big Smoke. Rounding up the layabouts and so on. Mooching round the dives. Gettin' in to watch the Spurs for nothin'. Watchin' the spivs in the Lane on a Sunday morning. Don't you ever feel a longin' to be back there?'

Britwell sighed. He punched a flat

patch in his pack and sank his head against it. 'Have you forgotten, Dipper, I've got a family of three waiting for me up the Bayswater Road! I get the longing all the time, when we're not shooting or being shot at.'

Marsh mumbled an apology, conscious that he had said the wrong thing. At that moment, Private Rigg touched him on the shoulder from behind.

'Mind if I ask you a question, Sarge?'

'No, go on, cock. What is it?'

'Well, I've often wanted to ask you,' Rigg went on, 'how did you come by a nickname like 'Dipper'?'

In spite of his weariness, Britwell chuckled. 'You shouldn't have asked him that, lad. He'll talk till the campaign's over. That's his favourite topic.'

Marsh looked from one to the other. 'Do you really want to know?' Rigg nodded. 'Well, there's not much to tell, really. Y'see, a dipper, in underworld language is a chap who dips into other people's pockets.'

'A pickpocket?' Rigg asked, unbelievingly. 'Surely you weren't a pickpocket,

Sarge. I always thought you were a policeman.'

'That's right,' Britwell put in mischievously. 'He was a pickpocket and the Metropolitan signed him on thinking he'd be able to catch the other dippers.'

'That wasn't it at all, Captain, and you know it,' Marsh remonstrated with mock severity. 'I'm not sure that last statement of yours doesn't come under the heading of defamation of character. I'll remember that, if we ever get back on the job.'

Rigg was really curious. He led the conversation back into a more serious vein.

'Well, I got the nickname in the Force,' the sergeant admitted at last. 'You see I caught so many pickpockets, I became a sort of expert.'

'But they work in gangs, don't they? It must have been very difficult to pick them out in a crowd when they were ready to operate.'

Marsh rubbed his nose thoughtfully. He glanced at Britwell, and then went on. 'Yes, it's true they work in teams. Three at once, usually. One bloke barges the mug, knocks him into another member of the team, who does the actual dip, and he hands on the wallet to a third chap, who walks away with it, and meets them later for the share-out.

'What made the job difficult was when the mob was smart enough to keep changing the third man — the one who went off with the lolly. Most of the regular dippers and their barging oppos were known to us beforehand. We had dossiers on them at the Yard, you see. Like I said, you had to keep an eye on the geyser who went off with the lolly. Usually it took two or three plain-clothes men to round up the team. They always followed their regular *modus operandi*. Some worked the crowded streets at rush hour, and others concentrated on working the rattler.'

A puzzled frown spread over Rigg's plump face.

He said: 'Here, hang on a minute, Sarge, you're getting a bit technical, aren't you? What's the rattler, a big dipper or something?'

'No, not exactly,' Marsh admitted,

grinning. 'The rattler's slang for the London Underground.'

Recognition broke over Rigg's face. 'Now I'm with you, Sarge. Some of them specialise in knocking off wallets in the underground.'

'That's right, chum. It's easier to jostle people down there. It's always happening. Many a time, the mug will have got right home before he realises his wallet's gone. And even then it might take him an hour to think out when and where it was lifted.'

The conversation ran on for another five minutes. At the end of that time, Marsh glanced at Britwell and saw that he had dropped off to sleep. He nodded at him, gave Rigg a cigarette, and started to tell him a few stories about Britwell's brilliant police work.

★   ★   ★

That night, the German gunners fired starshells over the Allies' beach positions. Illuminated like Blackpool seafront, the desperate troops were subjected to a devastating bombing by three waves of Heinkels. They fired back with everything they had. But they were not to escape unscathed. Another small supply dump went up, and one of the new trenches was blasted in by a near miss.

It was a night to forget.

The following morning, the hanging yellow dust-clouds were even thicker. In spite of all the efforts of the Allied Strategic Air Force, and the naval gunners in the bay, the Panzer divisions slowly closed with the beaches.

Half-a-dozen howitzers had been landed at dusk.

The senior American officers had a conference to try and decide how best they could be used.

'If the Panzers get much closer, they'll be blasted back into the sea, where they came from,' a grizzled colonel observed unhappily.

The engineer officer, who had contacted Lewis, was the only one to put forward any constructive suggestion.

He said: 'Why don't we be bold? Push the guns up to the road? After all, that pall of dust has hindered us quite a bit. It's time we tried to make use of it.'

The colonel glared at him across the dug-out table. Nobody else made any comment. 'It's all very well for you, Gurney, an engineer, to make such a suggestion. *My* boys would have to take the risks haulin' the darned guns up there. I figure it would be suicide. We've lost a lot of men already, and we ain't goin' to get any reinforcements in a hurry, so far as I can see. I think it's foolhardy.'

The Major of Engineers licked his lips. 'I know a guy who could get them out there in no time. He'd only need a hint.'

'Who is this guy?' the colonel asked, with heavy sarcasm. 'Don't tell me Errol Flynn's out from Hollywood to take charge here.'

'This guy I have in mind has no nerves. He already proved it yesterday when he filled in those pill-boxes up there.'

The colonel whistled. He became thoughtful. 'Say, you don't mean that big palooka — the Limey with the fighter's scars in his face?'

'I do, indeed,' the engineer assured him.

The colonel worked on a hollow tooth with a toothpick. 'If any guy could get 'em up there without getting himself blasted, that Limey could. Maybe it's worth a try.'

He sent a messenger to look for Dusty.

★   ★   ★

To his surprise, the messenger, warned to hurry, found Lewis still asleep in the trench. The big man, however, showed no animosity, when rudely awakened.

'Say, bud,' the G.I. began, apologetically, 'I hate to disturb you like this, but the colonel's got a king-sized job for you, on the cat you were operating yesterday.'

'That's o-kay, Yank,' Lewis replied, stretching and flexing his muscles. 'I'm just about ready to take some more of those Nazis apart.'

He ran down to the water's edge, sluiced his hands and face and followed the messenger obediently back to the colonel's dug-out. There, he was given full instructions.

197

First of all, the Navy was going to put a barrage just over the road. In the first lull, Lewis was to tow the number one howitzer into place on the road. If all was quiet, he was to signal with his left arm. When the signal was received, the American artillery boys were to rush up the beach and prime the gun ready for action.

After that, the operation was to be repeated quickly, with further help from the naval ships when necessary. The yellow haze was still thick, and with a little luck, the operation might well be a success.

The artillerymen asked a few questions, and then the colonel turned to Lewis. 'You quite happy with what you have to do, Lewis?'

'Sure, I'm ready Colonel when you are.'

The conference broke up and Lewis moved out and started up his machine. The first howitzer was quickly coupled up with a large split pin, and Dusty made his first run. The naval barrage was still on, and bright flame-tinged clouds were adding to the yellow haze.

Half way up the beach, Lewis turned in his seat, grinned back at the watchers and waved happily. He clattered on, over some fallen stones from a flattened wall. The naval shoot stopped just as he rocked forward onto the road. The pall of smoke and dust made him cough fitfully, but it did nothing to dampen his high spirits.

Jumping clear, he ran round the back, hauled out the heavy connecting pin with one savage jerk, waved his left arm wildly and clambered back on board, grabbing for his twin clutches.

'This is the life,' he muttered to himself. 'If only old Nipper was 'ere to see me now. Or Lucy . . .'

On the way back, he passed the apprehensive artillerymen as they scrambled after the howitzer. 'What you worryin' abaht?' he yelled derisively. 'There ain't no Jerries rahnd 'ere. It's like Scotland on a flagday.'

The latter remark had been one of Harris's favourite witticisms at one time. He had heard it so often, he remembered it.

'It's o-kay for you, Limey,' one G.I.

grumbled. 'You can pull out when you want to. When we get there, we gotta stay!'

'You got a chance to pick up a purple 'eart, though!' Dusty yelled back at them.

He swung the machine round in a generous arc, braked to a stop, and lit a cigarette while another field gun was hitched. Without more ado, he started the operation all over again. In quick time, five guns were taken up to the road. Each time, he parked the last one twenty yards further towards the south, so that when the fifth one was in place he was nearly a hundred yards away from his starting point.

It was at this stage that the unexpected happened.

Two German Mark VI tanks crept up the road from the south unobserved. So thoroughly absorbed was Lewis in his job that they remained unnoticed. Shells from a small calibre gun exploded right under the rear of his machine, blasting the last howitzer into twisted metal.

He leapt from his machine and hurled himself into the ditch on the land side of the road while the tanks were still firing from some three hundred yards away. The American artillerymen were quick to react. While the ill-fated bulldozer was gradually being pulverised, they swung round the first three howitzers and in a matter of seconds were making a spirited reply.

Three minutes later, as Lewis came out of the ditch and shot across the road to the gunners, crouching, the first tank succumbed in a flaming cloud.

Dusty Lewis was fighting mad again.

'Too bad about your cat, bud,' an N.C.O. observed.

'Never mind about the cat, mate!' Lewis yelled. 'Any of you blokes got a grenade on you?'

The N.C.O. passed him a couple, while the others strove rapidly to get the range of the second tank which was going about, intent on pulling out before it suffered a similar fate.

'Ta, mate,' Lewis said briefly.

Clutching the grenades in one huge hand, like a couple of apples, he slipped back beyond the ditch and went after the retreating tank at a loping run. It kept going at a steady twenty-odd miles per hour until it was three miles away. Then it stopped. But Lewis was a hard man to shake off. He had one great quality, and that was singleness of purpose. Although not in the peak of condition, he ran the three miles in a little over a quarter of an hour.

A young officer and one other soldier had quickly got out of the tank. The soldier was smoking and the officer was studying the beaches through glasses. They saw Lewis at the same instant as he saw them. He was not slow to react. In the split second it took them to decide whether he was a menace or not, he pulled up, breathing hard, hauled a pin out of the first grenade and took careful aim. In a pose quite like an American baseball pitcher, he paused for a whole second. Then, when he was sure the two Germans were both going to run for the same side of the iron-clad, he tossed the grenade towards them.

The soldier panicked. He knocked his officer off-balance as he scrambled to be the first back in the tank. They were both clawing themselves up the side when the grenade exploded within a yard of them. Both men crumpled, their anguished cries drowned by the explosion. Lewis, who was already moving up again, merely grunted. He ran on, anxious that the tank should not start up and outdistance him again. There were anxious cries from within, following the explosion. A head came into view, took in the scene, and disappeared again. Lewis was within five yards when the hatch dropped with a clang. He hurled himself over the intervening ground, scrambled up the machine from the back, and hauled the hatch open before it could be secured.

He pulled the pin out of the second grenade, eyed it sharply for a second and dropped it within. Then he closed the hatch and stood on it. Almost at once, the explosion jolted him off again. He picked himself up off the ground, chuckling wickedly. That would teach them to shoot up his 'dozer!

With a sigh, he started slowly back the way he had come. There was no doubt in his mind that the bulldozer was a total write-off. His spirits slowly sank. With no driving to do, Red Beach seemed suddenly unattractive again. He became aware for the first time that day of a gripping hunger. He felt he owed no special loyalty to anyone. Presently, he slipped off the road on the landward side and went in search of tomatoes and fruit.

14

That night, the Luftwaffe made an all-out attack upon the anchorage.

It was fortunate that the day before the Mediterranean Fleet, based on Malta, had been alerted. Although the gravity of the situation was kept from the ship's companies, commanding officers were fully aware that the Salerno assault was approaching a critical phase. It could quite conceivably develop into another Dunkirk, though on a smaller scale.

On the ground, the Germans, entrenched on commanding heights, gave back better than they received. Only air superiority, and the Navy could in any way redress the balance. About this time, the Tactical Air Force, centred on newly-acquired bases in the Middle East, and kept primarily for bombing and strafing German and French cities where military targets were situated, was switched to help combat the *Luftwaffe in Italy.*

At the same time, the capital ships of the Med Fleet were brought up to Salerno to give any help they could with their greatly experienced high-angled gunnery.

Without the help of the big ships, the smaller and more vulnerable of the assault ships might well have been rendered completely useless. The night was dark when the Luftwaffe started to fly over in regular waves, dropping their bombs from a great height.

Warspite and *Valiant* answered the challenge. Soon 6″ and even 15″ projectiles were bursting in and around the hostile formations. In the darkness these proved an awe-inspiring sight to friend and foe alike. Over a prolonged period, the big guns continued their onslaught. Every time a barrel was fired, the flame-licked back-lash of the gun illuminated the mounting and the superstructure.

The teeth of all the close company were jarred. In between the big explosions, and the accompanying roar, streams of sparks flew skyward and bright tracer laced the sky. Many enemy planes plunged on their last dive, and many Allied ships were hit, blazing for long periods and helping the enemy to pinpoint their attack.

Over a hundred sea-borne fighters had taken part at Salerno. At this stage, only about twenty of them were still airworthy. Most of them had been brought to the scene of operations in Woolworth carriers with narrow decks. This deck difficulty, coupled with the fact that the small carriers were only capable of doing eighteen knots flat out, was responsible for a troublesome and costly series of accidents.

Pilots lacking essential experience flew down to land-on at too great a speed. Many shedded their hooks, piled into the crash barriers, flew into the flight-deck parking areas, or — worse still — plunged straight over the side. As the fighter situation deteriorated, squadrons of reinforcements were flown ashore to an improvised landing-strip at a place called Paestum. They continued to operate from this landing-strip for several days, although at times they were under fire from German gunnery based in nearby olive and citrus groves.

In the early hours, a Liberty ship was hit by bombs.

It immediately caught fire, and the conflagration spread until an unfortunate landing craft, moored alongside, was also fired. A series of minor explosions in the well-deck soon had the crew in a panic.

The Senior Officer immediately flashed a signal for the L.C. to cast off and pull further out to sea. But the furnace-like well-deck made the ship a death-trap.

Fearful for their lives, the crew went over the side and scrambled aboard the larger vessel. The harassed skipper was calling them back through his loud hailer, when Rawson, riding at anchor quite close, decided to go to his aid. His engines were still warm and it did not take long to get under way.

The stricken L.C. was moored port side to the Liberty ship, facing inshore. L.T.C. 17 came about and went to pass her starboard side. Rawson knew the skipper. The two of them had been through a course of training together, and later had been members of the same flotilla in western Scotland. While the other skipper, Raystrick, tried to lure his engine-room crew back on board, other members of his crew were playing hoses on the well-deck from the Liberty ship's rail.

Rawson hailed him. 'Ahoy, there, Tubby! Stand by to secure a couple of lines over your stern. We'll tow you clear!'

Raystrick responded, glad of the assistance. Single-handed, he caught and secured two lines round bollards on his quarterdeck. Another explosion occurred forward.

'Get out of it, mate,' Rawson called without ceremony. 'And have your men cast her loose. Hurry it up, if you don't want to go up with her.'

No captain ever left his ship with such alacrity. One after another, the securing ropes were cast off from the Liberty ship. Rawson adjusted his telegraph and warned his messenger to keep an eye on the tow ropes. They held. Slowly, L.T.C. 17 hauled its sister ship clear of the Liberty ship's bulk. Rawson was worried.

Any time almost, the fire could spread to the L.C.'s high-octane petrol tanks.

The Senior Officer flashed another urgent signal, this time to Rawson. It said: *Tow her half a cable's length and endeavour to sink her.*

Signalman Joyce flashed an acknowledgement while Rawson sweated on his bridge in the full knowledge of the risks he was taking. The surface-air battle went on unnoticed. The two vessels had proceeded about a furlong when Rawson ordered his pom-pom gunners to stand-by. He wondered how many shells would be needed to speed the stricken L.C.'s end.

He was still fretting over the unpleasant task of having to sink her when the combustibles in the burning well-deck did the job for him. An explosion of greater fury than any of the previous ones finally blew open the great bow door.

Sea-water poured into the burning hold, and slowly she settled to her lasting resting place. The bearded skipper's throat was dry when he gave the order to cast her loose. There was nothing further he could do.

Meanwhile the sea-air battle dragged on.

★ ★ ★

Although he was no more than a mile or two from the Salerno coastal strip, the night-noises of the battle did not disturb Scoop Britwell. He was sleeping like a babe in the hayloft of a small mixed farm.

Even the cockerel at dawn did not break in upon his slumbers. Another hour passed before a round-eyed chubby Italian girl trotted across the yard from the house, opened the barn door, and crept up the ladder to the loft.

'*Signore* Britwell, it is time to wake up!'

She seized his shoulder by the flash and shook him with all the strength which a four-year-old can muster.

Britwell grunted, sniffed, shook his head, and finally blinked his eyes aggressively. The tiny olive face peered down at him intently. He let out his breath with a long sigh. 'Oh, Lucia, it's you! For a moment you frightened me.'

'You were frightened, *signore*?' repeated

the four-year old. 'But why? I did not pull faces at you.'

Britwell sat up suddenly. He laughed. 'Never mind, little one, you wouldn't understand.' He ran his fingers through straggly fair hair which was becoming overlong at the sides and back. Too long for the daytime heat of Italy in late summer.

'Violetta says breakfast is almost ready.'

'Then tell Violetta I shall be happy to eat it in five minutes, when I have gathered my wits.'

'What are wits?'

'I will tell you after breakfast. Run along now.'

The youngster scampered back the way she had come and Britwell rose slowly, followed her down the ladder and washed himself at a tap in the yard. After smelling at the air appreciatively, he wandered into the kitchen and put his arm round the plump shoulders of the woman, Violetta.

She had brown, flabby arms, a huge bust and abdomen, and was encased in a dark shapeless dress which revealed her as being pear-shaped. Her figure made her seem old. The eyes and hair, however, hinted at the truth. She was in her late thirties.

'Ah, *Signore* Britwell, you slept well, eh?'

Britwell assured her heartily that he had never slept better. He went over to a well-scrubbed wooden table and sat down, helping himself to a handful of walnuts.

In a huge black frying pan his breakfast was sizzling. It consisted of two pullets' eggs, four tomatoes and some fruit he had never heard of. Only a daily paper was needed to make this a normal breakfast, English style.

Britwell grinned to himself. He was seeing the great upper room in that building in Fleet Street where the *Daily Globe* was prepared for the presses. In his mind, he went over the various desks belonging to the specialist writers. He checked them carefully, accounting for those who had received their calling-up papers.

He wondered what old Dufrayne, his editor, had thought about his two despatches sent from Reggio. He hoped they were up to the high standard he had set for himself in wartime journalism.

The woman, Violetta, swept his food onto a large chipped plate and slapped it down in front of him. He sniffed at it appreciatively. Without more ado, he started to eat it. Violetta blew a wisp of hair out of her face, and sat back on a stool so as to enjoy seeing him demolish it.

Britwell glanced at her from time to time. He thought he had been very fortunate when he asked openly for food at this farm the previous day. He had stated from the start that he was English. This had won him a glass of wine and a handful of grapes. He decided to be even more confiding when he spotted the two children. He explained how he had brought *Signorina* Prucci from Potenza back to her native town of Battipaglia. At that stage, Violetta, the children's aunt had really warmed to him. She sensed his great interest in Marisa, and talked at great length about the girl, explaining what a fine teacher she was, and what a lot of hard work she had done with seven-year old Luigi, who had been slow to learn to read.

It was taken for granted that he would remain at the farm, resting and feeding himself for the whole of the day and — if he could be persuaded — to stay until the Allies had driven the Germans out of the area. He had accepted the offer of overnight hospitality with gratitude.

In the evening, the plump Violetta had told him more about Marisa, and he had opened up a little himself; enough to talk about his brother, Jack, anyway. He found his Italian improved in fluency with the easy practice.

When he had eaten the food, and made suitable suggestions as to its excellence, they talked for a while about the seesaw battle taking place westward on the beaches. Violetta was anxious for him to stay longer, but she could see that he was restless. Marisa had provided a second interest in his life, but he still wanted very much to meet up with Jack, and he was more than ever sure that his brother must be quite close.

He was lounging back smoking a cigarette when a youthful high-pitched whistle carried down to them from the slope at the back of the farm.

Violetta beamed. She said: 'Luigi, he comes, no?'

Britwell nodded. Luigi was the seven-year old lad who had been at Marisa's school until it was bombed. Since dawn he had been away on a self-imposed task of watching the valley road for signs of the Bosche.

The boy came skipping down the slope. He was barefooted. His lithe body was encased in a scrubbed and faded blue shirt and long trousers long since past their best and roughly shortened to an inch or two below his knees.

'*Signore* Britwell!' he called. 'I have great news for you!'

'I know,' Britwell said as the boy sprang in at the door, 'the Germans have surrendered and we can all rest easy.'

Luigi leapt across the room and pummelled him in the chest. 'You mock me!' he cried. 'But wait till I tell you.' Unable to keep the news any longer, he blurted it out. 'The Germans are retreating. They are moving back up the valley.'

'Are you sure?' Britwell queried, grabbing the boy's arm.

He squirmed free and jumped back a pace. 'Si, si, si, it is true. They retreat. Now, what do you say? Am I not the best spy in all Lucania?'

'The very best, Luigi,' Violetta put in. She caught him and hugged him to her ample bosom.

'Then it will be safe for me to move on,' Britwell observed thoughtfully.

Luigi's eyes twinkled mischievously. 'But there is a man in the tomato patch. He is eating his way across it.'

Violetta started. She turned the boy round, peering at him to read his true thoughts. Britwell started to his feet. The boy burst out laughing, unable to contain himself.

'*Diablo!*' Britwell bellowed. 'You are teasing me. It is untrue, I think.'

'It is true, it is true. Cross my heart. But — he is English!'

Britwell's interest quickened. The boy, full of his new knowledge, described the man in detail, down to his shoulder flashes which the war correspondent recognised as those of the Pioneer Corps. One Pioneer stood out in his memory, but he thrust that aside. It was too far away for it to be the man he had in mind, in spite of the fitting description.

The three of them swarmed out of the house and hurried to the tomato patch, closely followed by Lucia. There, the interloper stopped short at his breakfast, standing like a statue among the plants. He blinked hard, recognised Britwell from the time when they had crossed to Reggio together.

He came slowly forward to shake hands, his stubbly face pink through an unaccustomed blush and the tomato he had been eating. They led him back to the kitchen where he put himself outside a breakfast larger than the one eaten by Britwell.

Then, quite suddenly, he started to talk. He told how his first 'dozer had been buried in the cottages after Harris's death. And how the second one had finally been knocked out by the Mark VI tanks while he had been employed on

Red Beach. Britwell questioned him about his movements, revelling in the unusual story which the ex-fighter had to tell. This was copy of the first order.

It came as a complete surprise, however, when he learned that Lewis had moved up to Salerno in the same L.C.T. which had brought them across from Sicily, and that the 3rd Home Counties Commando had travelled with him. Lewis was not much good at describing people, but he remembered Tufty Britwell's name. There could be no mistake about it. Old Jack was here, at Salerno, on Red Beach.

When Lewis's narrative came to an end, Britwell gave him a cigarette, and put a proposition to him.

'Look here, Dusty, I'm searching for my brother, among other things. The Germans are pulling out now, and you haven't anything particular to do. Why not show me where you came ashore? That way I'd get to see my brother quickly. In any case, they'll probably have brought more machines ashore by now. You could be very useful if you took up driving again.'

Lewis' interest quickened. 'You think they'll 'ave more 'dozers now?' He watched Britwell's face, wondering if he was just saying that to get him to go.

'It stands to sense, doesn't it? There's lots and lots of jobs they just can't do without bulldozers. And the Yanks have dozens of them. They pour them out like Liberty ships — by the thousand! What do you say? Will you show me?'

Lewis wiped his greasy mouth on the back of his hand.

'O-kay, mate, you got yourself a guide.'

The two of them left within the half hour. Each had promised to return, if and when the opportunity arose. And both men sincerely hoped it would. Lewis had been taken with Violetta's cooking, and she had promised to teach him a little Italian if he came back. The idea pleased him.

Moreover, the boy, Luigi, had promised to walk into Battipaglia and tell Marisa that Scoop was fit and well.

They stepped out towards the sounds of gunfire as though they were going on a picnic.

15

In a couple of hours they reached the stretch of road to which Lewis had hauled the howitzers. Others had been brought up from the beach by then, and they were well secured and in good order.

The grizzled old colonel greeted Lewis warmly.

He said: 'Say, that Major of Engineers will sure be glad to see you back. He's got another cat down there, an' it's playin' up like a whore out of hell!'

The information cut short the talk. Lewis hurried Britwell down the beach, leaving him at every stride. Another air-raid developed over the shipping as they approached, but Lewis ignored it. His eyes were glued to another bulldozer, fresh out of the crate and gleaming with red paint. A puzzled G.I. was fiddling with something in the engine.

Scoop let him go. He made his own way over to the trench which had been reinforced by the commandos. To his surprise, he found it occupied by a bunch of G.I.s, resting up. There was no sign of British uniforms anywhere. The mystery was soon cleared up when he started to enquire after them.

An exceedingly tall, thin Lieutenant beamed down at him, his jaws working rhythmically on a wad of Chiclet. He soon wised him up.

'You want the Limey commandos, huh? Yeah, I know 'em. They moved south a piece at dusk yesterday. Headed for the Blue sector. Sure, you'll catch up with 'em o-kay. Shucks, that's o-kay. So long, now. Take it easy.'

Britwell paused for a few moments. He wanted to say goodbye to Lewis, but the big fellow was already totally immersed in getting to grips with the new machine. He had already forgotten Britwell's existence.

Scoop grinned at him. He moved off southwards, his footsteps brisk. Twenty minutes later, the Britwell brothers spotted each other while still a furlong apart. The sudden meeting was a warmly touching affair, witnessed by Dipper

Marsh and many of the men who had followed Tufty so loyally in the previous grim week.

The commandos were in high spirits. The news of the German withdrawal up the river valley had reached the lines just an hour earlier. The Home Counties men were under short notice to move off. For them, it was the end of hunkering in a damp trench, doing the work of the ordinary infantrymen. Along with men of the Reccy Corps, they had been chosen to form the spearhead of Allied troops to lead the attack against the mountain passes to the north.

'It's too bad we've got to move so soon after you've caught up with us, Harry,' Tufty observed with feeling.

'Don't let that bother you, Jack boy. I've seen no action worth mentioning since my captors were ambushed up Potenza way. I'm coming with you! There's no power on this beachhead could stop me.'

'We'll be glad to have you with us, Scoop. Gosh, it must be six months since I read one of your despatches in the old *Globe*.'

The speaker was Dipper Marsh. Scoop grinned at him good-humouredly. He knew the ex-detective from his crime-reporting days.

'Don't let that trouble you, Dipper. You're more than likely to figure largely in the next one!'

'Are you serious, chum?' Marsh asked, suddenly embarrassed.

'I've never been more serious, mate,' Scoop assured him. 'And a certain ex-pugilist who seems to know you all!'

'Dusty Lewis?' Tufty asked.

'None other. Come to think of it, you could do with old Dusty up front with you when you strike the passes. He brought me down to the beach a while ago. When I left him, he was just taking over a new bulldozer.'

'When we move off, we'll go that way,' Tufty decided. 'I'll see what I can do about getting him. After all, the Yanks owe us a favour or two for the last couple of nights.'

Down in the trench, a freckled commando waved the field telephone. 'Message from H.Q., Captain. Time for us to move out.'

Tufty Britwell hoisted his huge pack onto his back. He nodded. 'All right, Barton, tell them we're on our way.'

★ ★ ★

As the commandos moved out to become the spearhead of the British 10th Corps in the push to Naples, much hard fighting was going on around the perimeter of the Salerno plain.

In the Gulf, capital ships and cruisers, there largely as protection for the fifty Liberty ships now in use, were attacked by the new German radio-controlled glider bombs. H.M.S. Warspite was hit by one of these. Other naval units round about were surprised to see clouds of sulphurous smoke pouring from her funnels. It was deemed serious enough to remove her from the scene of action, and she was speedily despatched back to Grand Harbour, Malta, for repairs.

Although the German Panzer forces had withdrawn again up the valley to the east, very strong concentrations of the enemy still held that area in the vicinity of

Mount Eboli. To help dislodge them, five hundred planes — Mitchells, Marauders, and Flying Fortresses dropped a great weight of bombs in the Battipaglia area. In addition, two battalions of the 82nd Airborne Division, and a paratroop battalion were dropped behind the enemy.

Following a visit from General Alexander, 1,500 infantrymen were being brought over from Philipville by cruisers of the Royal Navy. Although the going was still hard, the desperate situation which had developed round the Salerno area had eased and the Allies had recovered confidence.

On the 16th of the month, the foremost patrols of the British Eighth Army, which had fought its way up from the toe, met and joined up with the southern outposts of the Fifth Army. This was one of the main reasons for the timely German withdrawal. It was to avoid becoming outflanked.

★ ★ ★

The commandos' first request to have with them Lewis and the bulldozer was refused on the grounds that he was needed to help cope with the ever-increasing stacks of material being brought ashore.

This could scarcely be argued against, and the commandos had to make do without him for a time. Within two days, however, they were brought to a full stop on a road leading out of the plain a little way east of Salerno town.

This road had been literally plastered with blocks, and countless small houses had been dynamited so as to render it impassable. For twenty-four hours, the commandos remained in the same position. A mile or so to the east, they were overlooked by high strong points on the hills, from which the enemy poured down upon them an incessant volume of shellfire.

Immediately to their right, between the road and the high ground, lay on area of woodland, mostly made up of scrub oak. In the daytime, the Home Counties men made two or three sorties into the woodland. Each time the patrols returned with the same story. It was completely devoid of human inhabitants.

And yet, in the night, the British

bivouac positions were subjected to a steady bombardment of small arms fire from that direction. Two or three mortars were in action against them. Towards dawn, another patrol went into the wood. The gunfire ceased before they had penetrated far, although they gave no sign of their presence. Again they could not find any sign of the enemy.

Much puzzled, Marsh brought out the last patrol half an hour after dawn. Being a detective by profession, drawing a blank touched his pride.

'I just can't understand it, Tufty,' he grumbled, when the two of them were alone together in their dugout. 'We scoured the whole area right up to the hill slopes and we never saw the slightest sign of Jerry.'

Britwell sluiced the dregs of his tea round the bottom of his mug. 'Well, somebody must have done the shooting. It certainly came out of the wood. And it was no dream. Otherwise we wouldn't be burying another twelve men. I don't mind telling you the blokes are pretty rattled by it all.'

Marsh knew he was right. It was one thing to be killed in action by an enemy you could see, or at least know the whereabouts of, but to be shot up by phantoms definitely had an unsettling effect.

'I'll go in again, if you like,' he volunteered unhappily.

'No you won't. I'm not blaming you at all. Sooner or later we shall get to the bottom of it. It's costly that's all. Both in manpower and in morale. We're going to dig ourselves in for a while and take it easy. I've sent back to H.Q. and said we can't do anything in the way of progress until we get bulldozers. One at least, and more if they can be spared. I only hope the G.O.C. fully realises the predicament we are in.'

After a scratch meal, the men spent an hour burying their comrades and putting up stones and suitable epitaphs. It was sad work, but it occupied them and took their minds off the frustrating knowledge that they could not go forward.

It was eleven a.m. when Dusty Lewis rolled up, unescorted, on his shiny red machine. He lost no time in getting out of the driving seat and making a swift reconnoitre of the position. Up the obstacled road, his bulky figure was spotted by the German rearguard. Three Spandaus opened up on him. He owed his life to the substantial road blocks which were causing all the delay.

Dodging and ducking from one to another, he finally got back to the commandos' positions. He took a proffered cigarette and slumped back in the dugout to enjoy it.

Marsh and Britwell were watching him closely. He was a difficult man to weigh up, but they felt sure he had come to some sort of decision. He did not keep them in suspense long.

'That road's pretty 'opeless, sir!' he said forthrightly. Incidentally, Tufty Britwell was the only officer he bothered to address as 'sir'. This compliment did not pass unnoticed.

'But you aren't saying that your bulldozer couldn't clear it?' the captain queried.

Dusty favoured him with a deprecating

smile. 'O' course it could clear it,' he said, as though stating the obvious, 'but it would take a time. Yard by yard, with that weight of concrete and broken stone, it'd take an age. A tortoise would get to Naples before us, an' it's speed that counts, so the general was tellin' me.'

Dipper's curiosity knew no bounds. 'But you've got an idea in the back of that granite skull of yours, Dusty, I'm sure. Let's know what it is, for goodness' sake. We can't do with *you* going all bloody mysterious on us.'

'We got to get off the road,' Dusty explained simply.

'Through the wood?' Tufty suggested, fingering his chin.

Dusty nodded. 'Sure, through the wood. There's lots o' trees about, I know, but it'd be a damned sight quicker than tryin' to clear the road.'

Marsh and Britwell exchanged thoughtful glances.

'He could be right,' Marsh remarked.

Lewis looked hurt. He rubbed his low forehead with the scarred knuckles of his right hand. 'Twenty-four hours! One day an' I'll 'ave you through that wood an' back onto the road. Besides, your men would be safer in there from shellfire off the 'ill slopes!'

Tufty marvelled at the big man's grasp of the situation, but he thought it wise to inform him of the mysterious attacks which had been perpetrated from that area. Lewis was in no way put off.

'If you 'ave your boys follow me up, they'll soon get to the bottom of that.'

He was very persuasive. Britwell went along with his idea. Leaving a score of men in the trenches to return a token fire when the enemy on the hillside bombarded them, he had the rest of his squad prepare to move off after the 'dozer.

Lewis spat on his hands, and started up. He tore into the scrub oaks as though they were a labour of Hercules. Behind him, the commandos moved up slowly. They were very wary at first, but when no sort of attack developed from the wood, the ex-fighter's workmanlike approach to his task began to heighten their spirits.

It was slow work for them, moving after

him yard by yard; occasionally helping in some small way, by lopping off awkward branches or hauling trees further to one side. By three p.m. they were almost half-way through. At this stage, Britwell called a halt. After placing sentries at strategic points, they settled down to a meal.

Lewis, needless to say, ate more than any other man. He took a lot of good-humoured chaffing in the spirit in which it was meant. While they were still eating, Scoop returned.

He had been away since dawn, doing a lone scouting effort towards the town of Salerno. Although he had not been nearer than a couple of miles, the view through his binoculars had clearly showed the Allied forward patrols in the outskirts of the town.

Helping himself to a plateful of stew, he sat down beside his brother. 'Well, it looks as if you're making progress at last, Jack. I suppose the big fellow is at the back of this wood effort.'

They looked across to where Lewis was silently munching his food in solitary splendour beside the bulldozer.

Tufty filled him in on what had happened. Scoop listened carefully, nodding now and then, and occasionally asking a question. Having cleared his plate, he burped softly. 'You know that chap deserves a medal. He's worth any ten men behind one of those machines.'

Dipper Marsh poked his teeth with a match. 'You're right, of course, Scoop, but I've got a feeling old Lewis would be offended if they offered him one.'

They were still discussing the fighter when he rose slowly to his feet, threw out his ample chest and stomach and rubbed them down contentedly. He stretched hugely and turned to grin at the men who were still eating.

'Ain't no 'urry for your boys to get started, sir. I won't run away!'

Four score pair of eyes watched him as he set the machine in motion again. The roar of the diesel titan filled the woodland. Working systematically, he tore into the trees again. One fell away to the right and the next to the left.

'I reckon the Fourteenth Army could

use him, in the Burma jungles,' Scoop opined.

'Burma'd be an open plain in a couple of months,' Marsh added.

They talked on, and Lewis opened up a gap between himself and them of some fifty yards. His face brightened as he came to a wide glade. He knocked out one more tree and rolled the machine forward.

He was chuckling to himself and thinking the commandos would have to run shortly when his caterpillar tracks clattered with a metallic noise. Leaning first to one side and then the other, he tried to make out what was causing the sudden change. It was the first time he had shown any concern since taking over the red monster. He was still trying to figure out what had happened when the front end of the machine dipped down suddenly. There was a rending of metal and it plunged down, into the earth.

Yelling with rage, he pitched down some thirty feet into darkness, hauling up on the bottom of the concealed pit with a jolt which jarred the back of his skull against the metal frame.

All around in the gloom, he became aware of movement accompanied by alien shouts of alarm. The machine was still in motion. It rocked forward over human bodies while he strove to accustom his eyes to the sudden darkness.

In a matter of seconds he began to make out faint lights. Somewhere to his right, a machine-gun opened up on him. With a roar of rage, he turned the 'dozer in that direction, ploughing forward until the gunner went under his scraper, almost cut in two.

Harsh orders rang in his ears. He yelled out himself realising that he had fallen into the hideout of the phantom enemy. Feet rushed nearer above the top of the depression.

'Where are you, Dusty?' a hoarse voice yelled.

'Over 'ere, mate,' he yelled back.

'Stay right where you are, then!'

He stopped the machine, scrambled clear and scooped two struggling figures together in his arms. Bones gave under his hug. His victims screamed in dire pain, then went inert. He dropped them to one side, fell over a rifle, and seized it for a club. The place was in a chaotic uproar. There were four exits from under the camouflaged, corrugated iron cover. Men rushed to each of them and scrambled to get out.

Sharp and persistent bursts from Sten and Bren guns told where their efforts to get clear failed. Above ground, the startled commandos were working with precision.

Upwards of forty men withered before their concentrated fire before a wary, blinking officer managed to scramble into the bright sunlight behind a dirty handkerchief tied on a rifle. Slowly, the warren emptied. Another fifty men came out with hands raised and surrendered.

They were lined up, hands on heads, along the cleared corridor. Still menacing with their weapons, the commandos whispered to one another.

Britwell made a swift count and came up with a further surprise. He turned to his brother: 'There were more Jerries down there than in the whole of our party, Harry!'

Scoop nodded. He was thinking that the Germans could have slipped out in the night and wiped out the decimated commando, if they had known. Thanks to old Lewis, things had turned out for the best once more.

A score of commandos escorted the sorry Germans back to their borrowed trucks on the far side of the road where they had been held up for so long. When they returned, Lewis had covered another furlong beyond the depression. In the early evening, he led the way into open country again, closely followed by the others.

The road was one hundred yards away, and its surface — for a useful stretch — was comparatively clear. Only a wooden, barred gate separated them from it. Lewis, disdaining to have the gate opened, neatly put his rammer through it. He moved easily onto the highway, dropping the wooden fragments carefully to one side.

Marsh was muttering to himself as he

stepped out onto the firmer ground. 'If I read all this in a boys' comic, I wouldn't believe it!'

Scoop remained silent. He had to write about it, for adults to read who were far from gullible. He hoped they would not think it too far-fetched.

16

After the remarkable events in the woods just described, the speed of the general advance towards Naples slowed considerably. Although the Germans had withdrawn in the Salerno area, it was not because of any desire to avoid action, but simply to prevent their forces from being outflanked by the Eighth Army.

The Allied air forces and navies continued to play a large part in neutralising the German advantage of being able to choose the ground on which to fight their rearguard actions. The Home Counties Commando, alternating with another similar unit, and their counterpart, the United States Rangers, maintained their steady pressure on the enemy.

Much stubborn fighting took them out through the two mountain passes to the north, into the plain of Naples. And there, although the terrain had altered, the fighting was just as desperate. While the above-mentioned troops maintained fighting contact, mobile columns of both the British 10th Corps and the United States 6th Corps were able to assemble behind them and fan out into the plain.

Many bridges had been blown in the plain area. In order to find one intact, the Home Counties Commando had to trek ten miles inland. They found it well covered by German units on lower ground beyond it. Throughout a whole morning, mortars poured a steady shell fire onto it at regular intervals. While his men rested in cover, Tufty Britwell, who was still miraculously unscathed, held a short conference with his brother, Scoop, who had loyally stayed with them, and Sergeant Dipper Marsh.

About midday, the three of them were seated on the concrete floor of a pill-box on the near side of the bridge, which had had its top blown off.

'Well, what do you make of it?' Scoop asked soberly.

'If you ask me, there's anything from fifty to a hundred Jerries in the woods opposite making good use of the trees for cover. They'll take a bit of shifting. To say nothing of that mortar outfit raking the bridge.'

Dipper had sounded down in the mouth.

After over three weeks of strenuous fighting, this was to be expected. The Commando was now reduced from four hundred to a bare sixty fighting men. Only one officer and three N.C.O.s had survived that far. The survivors' expectation of life could not be more than a few days.

Scoop had his glasses to his eyes. He was studiously scanning the cratered smoking top of the volcano, Vesuvius, a couple of miles or so to westward. He blew a cloud of cigarette smoke past the other two. Lowering the glasses, he said: 'I know how you blokes must be feeling. All of you must at times wonder whether any of your unit will survive to reach Naples. I think you will. Moreover, I think you've done a very fine job so far. Being a spectator, I can see the whole issue more or less in perspective. Consider the distance still to go. Old Vesuvius is right by us, that means that

242

Naples is no more than twenty miles away. Make no mistake, Jerry will have this weighed up. Any time now we shall be hearing the demolitions when they start to wreck the harbour.'

He paused, letting his gaze rest on each man in turn.

'I'm not a military man, but I think this bridge can be crossed. It must be crossed, for the sake of your men's morale. It's the only bridge standing in the area. One thing I've noticed this morning which might help. The mortars are firing at fixed intervals of ten to fifteen minutes. I may be wrong, but that suggests to me that they haven't any clear view of the bridge! Now, supposing I'm right, it should be possible to cross the bridge without getting tangled up with the mortars, provided the squad gets over in less than ten minutes. If I'm right, then it's just a matter of coping with the riflemen and machine-guns. What do you think?'

Tufty's lined face was rendered less formidable by an engaging smile. He was staring at his brother with frank admiration.

'You know that's pretty good reasoning on your part, Harry,' he remarked, with deference. 'As far as the mortars are concerned I came to exactly the same conclusion. *I* think the bridge could be taken. What we need is to keep the German infantry busy by continuous return fire from this bank while a sizeable body pushes over the bridge right on the tail of a mortar attack. One thing we could do to find out, though, before we attempt the crossing. We want to know fairly accurately where the mortars are firing from.'

Marsh looked as if he hated pouring cold water on the scheme. He said: 'I think your plan is pretty good, but if you leave, say, ten men on either bank to return a steady fire, that only leaves two-score to make the push, initially. Would that be enough?'

Tufty massaged his tired face with campaign-roughened hands. 'It will be enough, depending on two things. Firstly, that the two-score get some sort of inspiration to go ahead. It means I'll have to be up there in front, leading them, of course. But that's my job. Secondly, we need the right N.C.O. to bring across the rearguard without getting caught by the mortars. That's where you come in. Failing this scheme, we have to sit back and wait for the artillery to come up.'

'Why don't we take a walk upstream and try to locate the mortar point, then?' Scoop asked, enthusiastically.

'Why don't we?' Tufty echoed, scrambling to his feet. 'Dipper, you go and detail the men to keep up a steady fire on both sides of the bridge. Soon as you've done it, come after us.'

Side by side, the two brothers walked off together. The rest of the men had become accustomed to seeing them together. The resemblance was marked. They were both about the same height and colouring. The only noticeable difference was in the extra weight which Tufty carried across the shoulders. And, of course, the large sunglasses, which Scoop wore most of the time.

Taking a circuitous path, they approached the side of the river some two hundred yards further east. There, with binoculars ready, they waited for the next mortar attack. It came about twelve minutes after the previous one.

'I think we can count on ten minutes' grace when we go forward, provided we don't stir up too much noise,' Tufty opined.

'Hello, there goes the first,' Scoop exclaimed, as the first mortar projectile fell in an accurate parabola on the far bridge approach.

Both of them raised their glasses. They watched and listened while five other projectiles sailed after the first.

'It's two to three hundred yards north-east of the bridge, I'd say,' the captain said.

'On low ground, probably in a clearing,' the journalist added.

'You're wasted as a civvy, Harry.'

Just as he spoke, a rifle shot rang out from the trees opposite. With a disturbing groan, Jack Britwell slowly slumped to the ground. Cursing, Scoop dropped to his side. Scarcely daring to look into his brother's face, he dragged him back into cover with all speed. There, he looked him over anxiously. He was out cold and there was blood seeping down the left side of his head. A closer look revealed the fact that it had only been a graze along the temple. But it had been a near thing!

Scoop pulled out Jack's field-dressing and applied it to the wound. He was just finishing bandaging the head when Marsh dropped down beside him.

'How — how is he?'

'Just a graze, Dipper. Another inch, though, and it could have been fatal.'

The detective sighed with relief. 'We'll have to put off our little scheme, after all.'

Scoop rounded on him. 'Oh no we won't! It'll go off as planned!'

'But how can it, Scoop?' Marsh protested, his voice full of anguish.

'Because *I'm* going to lead the push across the bridge. And don't argue!'

Scoop's suggestion silenced Marsh. He stepped back, weighing up the unheard of suggestion. At first he thought his brother's wound had turned his head a bit. But Scoop was quite serious. Marsh could tell this by the way he was preparing for the job. He was carefully removing Jack's three-pipped tunic and wriggling into it himself.

'It'll be a fine thing if I have to write Scoop Britwell's obituary notice,' Marsh remarked, after a pause.

He was not happy about the new arrangement, but Scoop could tell that he would help it along.

'If it'll make you feel better, I'll tell the men — give them a chance to back down!' the journalist offered. 'And don't worry about what Harry will say. I'll fix it with him later. You'd better send a man over to look after him for the time being. Meantime, let's get cracking! And don't forget to follow us up smartly!'

After a last glance at Tufty's fallen figure, the two of them moved off back to the bridge approach. Scoop stepped along to the rear of the men detailed off to follow his brother. He cleared his throat to get their attention. They turned, eager for explanations and action. In spite of the family resemblance and the borrowed tunic, the sun glasses gave him away and brought startled glances from them.

He said: 'Men, you all know me by now. I'm your officer's brother. He was winged by a bullet just now — nothing serious, but enough to put him out of action for a while.

'Before he was sniped we worked out a plan one which ought to be put into operation without delay. It'll take his place just for this one job because I know the plan. There's only one thing to be settled. Will you follow me?'

Scoop studied the baffled, war-weary faces with their dark-ringed eyes, fatigue lines and chin stubble. Was he asking too much? A familiar face held his gaze.

Private Rigg said: 'I'm game if the others are . . . sir. We know your brother has a lot of confidence in you.'

'Count me in,' Private Barton, of the freckled face, added.

After that, there was a general murmur of agreement. Scoop relaxed and grinned. 'I think Tufty would approve, and I promise you there'll be no comebacks. Here's what we do, then. As soon as the next mortar barrage is over, I'm going forward. You men follow me about ten yards behind. Keep going forward. Fire back at anything you see. Be on the alert, that's all.'

Scoop went nearer to the bridge parapet and crouched there. Behind him, the two-score men checked their weapons and grenades. He concentrated on willing himself into the right frame of mind for what lay ahead.

Three minutes later, the mortars started firing again. He counted, one, two, three, four, five . . . and then he could not wait any longer. Just before the sixth exploded, he was on his feet, stepping onto the bridge and waving the men up behind him.

As he stepped forward unhesitatingly, the men in the rear kept pace with him, their eyes occasionally straying to the luminous patch on the back of the tunic which they had followed up Bagnare beach. The patch gave them confidence in the man. None of them was worried about the switch.

Scoop's face wore a strained grin as he stepped it out, wondering if the Germans might this time fire on the bridge seven times instead of six. As the seconds slipped by, punctuated by regular rifle and machine-gun exchange across the river, he knew they had not.

Half a minute dragged by with the steady footsteps approaching the middle of the structure. '*The Jerries must be blind not to see us*,' he muttered. Then the opposition opened up.

Spandau machine-guns began to throw twin jets of bullets up the bridge towards them. Steeling his nerves, he forced his mind to try and pinpoint their positions. He had with him three grenades, and Tufty's heavy Bren gun. This latter was already making his arm ache.

He brought it up, and sprayed the far bridge approach in a wide arc; an arc which would have been far wider if he hadn't held onto the weapon so tightly. The back of his neck tingled as the feet following him broke their steady momentum. Two grenades, quickly followed by a third, sailed through the air over his head. He hoped the marksmen did not suffer from nerves. On one occasion in his youth, he had been hit at the back of the neck by a cricket ball thrown in by a nervous fielder.

Rifle bullets were ricocheting off the

bridge stanchions as the three grenades exploded. Two of them landed off to the left, disturbing the rhythm of rifle fire. The other flew in a greater arc, bursting yards into the trees. As a direct result, one of the Spandaus ceased firing abruptly.

'Don't take your eyes off that thicket,' he shouted over his shoulder. 'The gun may be intact!'

A bullet pinged off his borrowed tin hat, knocking it slightly off centre. Fifteen yards to go and a man close behind coughed, and staggered, falling in his tracks. Nobody stopped to give him aid.

Scoop quickened his pace, with a mounting anger the driving force. He pulled out the first grenades, which had been tucked down Tufty's tunic. *The main thing is to get it away smartly, once the pin's been drawn*, he was thinking, *even if the aim's bad!*

He nipped out the pin with his teeth, as he had seen so many others do. A quick lean back, an extending of the right arm, and a swift throw in from the boundary. Watching it fly through the air, he stopped walking without noticing. Straight and true, the grenade flew into a thicket right ahead. He felt gratified when a German figure slowly slid into view, falling into the cloud of dust and smoke.

He had killed his first enemy. This was to trouble him later, but not then.

He started walking again. Now, he was clear of the structure. Without waiting to be told, the men fanned out behind him, trotting for the trees, never taking their eyes off the objective.

'When you've cleaned out this pocket, keep with me to the right!' he shouted.

He was about to add that they must get after the mortar crews with all speed when a sharp pain knifed into his right side, above the hip bone. He opened his mouth wide and breathed out hoarsely.

He broke into a run, but it seemed as if one of his legs had suddenly become shorter than the other. He slipped to his knees beyond the first trees. The Bren slipped from his hands. To his surprise he found three dead Germans within a few feet of him. Spasmodic bursts of fire were going on all around him. The noise sounded slightly unreal. There was a dizziness in his head which he could not account for.

Two commandos sprang past him. One of them dodged back again and came over to him.

'Keep moving, man,' Scoop remonstrated. 'What the hell are you stopping for at a time like this?'

Ignoring him, the man bent closer, concern showing in his eyes. 'Are you all right, sir?' he asked quietly.

Scoop nodded. A sudden burst of Spandau fire put the war mask back in place on the man's face. He trotted off, showing a lethal expression which his wife would not have known.

Five minutes later, Marsh led the other score of men across the bridge at the run. He had seen Scoop go down, and he almost pitched over him in the rush to reach his side.

'My God, are you all right, Scoop?'

Britwell's right hand was sticky with blood. The glance he bestowed upon Marsh seemed puzzled, as though everything was unreal.

'The mortars. Two to three hundred

yards, north-east. Low ground,' Scoop muttered.

Marsh stopped one of his men and thrust a field dressing into his hands. 'Here,' he ordered, 'fix up Mister Britwell's wound, then follow on.'

The detective gave one more anxious glance back as he hurried on after his men. Fifteen minutes later, the mortar crews were eliminated. The bridge area was cleared of the enemy.

17

About twenty-four hours after the Home Counties Commando had fought its way over the last bridge obstacle on the way to Naples, the Allied navies were standing off the all-important port, hoping to force an entrance.

Another factor had come into play, complicating the plans of the rival forces. The rains had started. The ships' companies were performing their tasks in sea-boots, oilskins and sou' westers. Coming at the end of the arduous action on the way to Naples, it tended to make all personnel short-tempered and nervy.

For upward of three hours, the capital ships had plastered the environs of the harbour with high-explosive shells of varying calibre from 16″ downwards. The obstinate German engineers made no attempt to clear out. They hung on, blasting away with demolition charges which added hugely to the destruction caused by the Allies.

The N.O.I.C. was in quandary. Under high-angle and surface fire cover, the minesweepers had gone in close to perform their hazardous task. Upwards of a score of mines had been brought to the surface by the sweeps and detonated. But when the sweepers came out again, they brought with them depressing news.

The harbour entrance was blocked almost to water level by the bows of a sunken ammunition lighter. This was confirmed by three forty-knot motor topedo boats which raced in to check the information. The news spread round the assembled ships, dampening the spirits of the crews with greater effect than the sheet rain and the hazy atmosphere.

The talk in the wardrooms and messdecks was that small advanced parties of foot soldiers were within a mile or two of the town's outskirts. Leg-weary and battle-fatigued as they all were, they needed the support of the navy more than ever before.

L.C.T. 17, and upwards of a dozen ships like her, swung slowly at anchor, trying to work out for themselves the possible outcome of the Naples operation. As they were not required for bombardment purposes, time hung on their hands. Watching the bigger fighting ships doing their shoots soon palled as a spectacle.

About two in the afternoon, Lieutenant Rawson relinquished his damp, slippery bridge for the claustrophobic two-bunk wardroom, which he had had to himself all the trip. It was good to slip out of the wet outer garments and have them hung up in the galley to dry out for a while.

But one could not settle in such circumstances. One could only lie back on the bunk and rest the body's tired muscles. Human dynamo though he was, Rawson would have admitted freely if asked, that the Naples lark had taken it out of him. His facial muscles were sagging under his beard. This was something he had never experienced before. Furthermore, on the previous day, he finally got round to trimming his beard for the first time on the trip. To his surprise, he had discovered here and there, a few silver hairs among the brown. His temples were beginning to sparkle with odd silver hairs, too.

The discovery was disquieting to say the least.

Puffing furiously at a cigarette, he turned sideways and peered thoughtfully at a group photograph of his wife and kids. They seemed a whole world away. His mind groped back to their home in Worcestershire. It came as something of a surprise when he remembered the massive padded armchair in their sitting-room, waiting for his return. Behind it, from ceiling to floor, was a tall set of bookshelves which he had constructed himself. He reflected that he had not read a book, except for the *Mediterranean Pilot* and other Naval reference books, in over eighteen months.

He wondered if reading would be a lost art with him after all this. For a chap who could get through four library books in a week at home, this was a staggering thought.

Rawson groaned out loud. He lit another cigarette from the butt of the other. Where was all this conjecture getting him? Nowhere. War was war, and war was here! And he was in it. He ought to be pleased he was still alive and uninjured, instead of moping over a few white hairs and the loss of the reading habit.

For a few moments more, he watched the tiny electric bulk-head fan whirl his smoke about, then he made an effort to pull himself together. He had to have company. It was bad being without his Number One all this time.

He called out in his usual booming voice. 'Scotty!'

The grimy, unhappy able-seaman saddled with the cooking appeared in the doorway in soiled white trousers, vest and apron. He was scouring a pan. 'Yes, Skipper?'

'Nip up on deck and ask Petty Officer Jones to come down and have a word with me, there's a good chap!'

The cox'n left the upper deck gratefully. His peaked cap was saturated and twice its normal weight. In addition, his best white cap-cover had shrunk and was pulling the cap out of shape. He hauled off his cap, and dropped it thankfully onto the tiny folding writing table.

'What-ho, sir,' he said, with a brightness he did not feel, 'want me to help you write up the log, or something?'

'Sit yourself down, Swain, and don't be so bloody flippant,' Rawson ordered. 'The rain I can stand, but a garrulous Welshman sounding off at the same time is the Pygmalion limit. Have a fag.'

Jones slid out of his oilskin and dropped thankfully on the spare bunk.

'What's the buzz?' Rawson asked briefly.

'Buzz, sir? There aren't any buzzes. The boys have run out of ideas. I'd never known them so chokka on the mess-deck. The calendar hasn't been changed for a week, and it looks as if Jane Russell is going to be the duty beauty for the rest of the trip. It's a pity in a way. She's a favourite of mine. As it is, some bright mateloe has been trying out his artistic tendencies on her, and I can assure you she hasn't been improved.'

'That's bad, as you say,' Rawson replied quite seriously.

The practice of showing big coloured pictures of cuddlesome beauties was a regular feature of messdeck life in most ships. When the men grew tired of looking at them, things had to be really bad.

'What do you reckon can be done about that submerged barge in the harbour entrance?' Rawson went on seriously.

Jones studied his face to make sure he expected a reply. The blocked entrance was certainly a facer. He was glad he didn't have to solve the problem. Being a petty officer was sufficient responsibility for him.

His thoughts wandered over their various landings in the land of sunshine, and the men they had been instrumental in putting ashore.

'Now if it was a blockage on land, the problem would be easy,' he opined. 'That big ex-fighter we keep meeting up with could tackle the job on his own, with a bulldozer. But under the sea, well, I just don't know. You got any ideas, sir?'

Rawson carefully removed a shred of tobacco from his lower lip. 'Why shouldn't it be bulldozed out of the way by a ship?' he suggested.

Jones's ginger brows shot up. 'What sort of a ship, Skipper?'

'This sort,' Rawson explained. He tapped the bunk beneath him with a stubby forefinger.

Jones stubbed out his cigarette, his mind working on the new idea. 'We only draw eight feet. Would we have the draft to shift it?'

'According to the buzz, the barge's bows are only a yard below the surface. We could touch it all right.'

'It might mean sacrificing the ship, sir.'

'I know,' Rawson replied soberly. 'But it could stop the whole operation from becoming a fiasco. What do you think?'

'Let me get this straight, sir. Are you suggesting that *we* try and shift the obstruction in L.C.T. 17?'

'I'm suggesting just that.'

'If you say so, sir, I'll back you, of course. Will you ask the ship's company first?'

'Do you think it would be best?'

'Might be a nice gesture on your part, sir.'

263

'Right then, I'll do it. Have all hands who can be spared muster in the messdeck in ten minutes.'

★   ★   ★

It was not often that the hands were mustered in a small busy ship like the L.C.T. Three men were dozing in their hammocks when Jones rounded them up. Besides the skipper and himself, there were present Jock Dodd, the P.O. Motor Mechanic, two stokers, two signalmen, a wireless operator, and three able seamen.

They hung about, in rolled down overalls and grimy shorts, tired but curious. Rawson, bareheaded, his scant hair flattened tonsure-fashion round his crown, put them into the picture as fully as he could. Then he explained his suggestion.

In conclusion, he said: 'Now I think you've all known me long enough to know that I wouldn't suggest a thing like this just to try and win a blooming medal for myself. Perish the thought. And seeing you would all be in some danger, I'm asking you what you think before I go any further in the matter. The Swain is the only chap I've spoken to so far. Now, what do the rest of you think?'

After a pause, the senior engine-room rating spoke up. 'The condition of the engines leaves a lot to be desired. If there has to be a sacrifice of a ship, I'd say this one has done its whack. Even if we don't attempt this job, the ship'll be needing a prolonged docking to have the engines seen to. I'd say it'd be cheaper to scrap her and have a new one.'

Dodd scratched away at his oily chin stubble with broken finger-nails. He went on: 'As regards danger, Skipper, that's not altogether new to us, is it now? On ordinary operations we could take a bomb through the bottom of the well-deck any time, or be blasted on some hostile beach. I think I've said enough. I'm with you, if you want to try it.'

One or two of the others murmured in agreement, and a wag suggested it might be a short cut to a bit of shore-time, which was overdue. Officer and crew laughed easily in each other's presence. A little of the old excitement was back in the ship.

'All right, men, thanks for your confidence,' Rawson said gratefully. 'I'll put the suggestion to the Flag Officer. He may think I'm up the pole, of course, in which case we'd better not get built up on it.'

Five minutes later, Signalman Joyce flashed a contact signal to the flagship. He began his message, which went as follows

L.C.T. 17 to Flag Officer. Request permission to attempt unblocking of harbour mouth with this ship.

The reply was slow in coming. Joyce called it out and Rawson wrote it down on the pad. It said:

F.O. to L.C.T. 17. Your suggestion under consideration.

Rawson scratched his beard with the pencil. He muttered: 'Well, the old boy hasn't written it off as ridiculous.'

★　★　★

Meanwhile, in a muddy stretch of plain, between Vesuvius and Naples, the Home

Counties Commando had again been brought to a halt. Huddled in gas capes, they were lying and kneeling in a plantation of scrub oak two hundred yards from a walled vineyard.

Behind the walls of the vineyard, three or four score Germans were firmly dug in. They had fought off two previous attempts to dislodge them by a force now reduced to fifty fighting men. Gunfire had become spasmodic. Both sides were conserving their ammunition.

The coming of the rains had affected the land forces far more than the navies. For more than a day it had poured down upon them, steady, persistent and drenching. The flat land, which should have provided easier going, had been churned into soft, yielding, treacherous mud. No really heavy weight could guarantee to keep going on it, and a truck without any ballast skated frenziedly from side to side, partially out of control.

Under two gas capes, supported on rifles, with the bayonets plunged into the ground, the Britwells and Dipper Marsh were huddled together unhappily. Tufty had a bandage round his head. He had recovered quickly from the flesh wound sustained during the bridge encounter. His loss of blood had been negligible. Scoop, with a slightly deeper wound in his side, had lost more blood. But he had insisted on keeping up with the party at all times. In a way, the bad going had helped him. It had slowed the feet of the fit men down to his own weakened gait.

'I can feel this rain right through to the marrow of my bones,' Marsh grumbled.

Scoop's bandages were becoming damp, but he did not mention this. Instead he said: 'It reminds me of a day up Snowdon years ago. Mist and rain went straight through a raincoat and a cape worn on top of it. I'll bet they never mention this weather in the holiday brochures on Sunny Italy.'

'How do we get out of this damned hole, that's what's worrying me,' Tufty said, with some fervour.

'What we really want is that good fairy on his bulldozer,' Scoop chipped in with unfelt heartiness.

'You're asking for the moon, Harry.

Lewis has been gone two days or more. Judging by the way that workshop was shaping, his machine will still be under repair when the war's over.'

'You're wrong mates, and to prove it I'm 'ere!'

The three of them could not have been more startled by the new voice. They knew it so well. Nobody could imitate Dusty Lewis's husky, pebble-in-the-mouth speech.

There he stood, not five yards behind them, muffled in his gas cape, beside a tall tree. 'You got any jobs you want done,' he said, 'the old machine's back in service.'

Dusty dropped to his knees beside them, and submitted to have his right hand pumped up and down energetically.

'One thing I like about you, chum,' Tufty enthused, 'is the way you turn up when we can't do without you.'

He pointed out the vineyard wall behind which the Germans were sheltered.

'We've tried everything to shift them, but we can't do it on our own. H.Q. sent a signal to the Navy a couple of hours back, but there's been no sign of a shoot yet. I think they've forgotten. By what we can hear they've got their hands full out at sea.'

Lewis assessed the situation, chewing delicately on a large bunch of purple grapes. 'I can knock out a gap in one go,' he decided. 'You'll 'ave to give me plenty of coverin' fire, an' some of your blokes would do well to creep up behind me. What do you say?'

'I'll alert the boys,' Tufty said. 'We'll start in ten minutes. I'll go in behind you with five volunteers.'

'You won't, you know,' Marsh said, frowning. 'If anything happens to you, this outfit will be officerless, and that means leaderless. Their morale will hit an all-time low.'

Tufty was about to protest when Scoop spoke out. 'He's right you know, Jack. Let him lead the volunteers. There'll be plenty more fighting before they give in. Too much, I'd say.'

Tufty gave in with an ill-grace. Ten minutes later, the commandos started to plaster the hundred-yard long wall with Brens. Lewis, on his machine, raced through and past them. The fire curtain split around his machine. Rocking and plunging, and making light work of the slippery mud which fouled up all other vehicles, he careered at the wall. Some two or three Germans hazarded a quick look through holes in the wall. Each of them promptly stopped a bullet before he could inform his comrades of what he saw.

Marsh and five other men, bent and shuffling, slithered after the big machine, taking what cover it afforded. At full speed, the giant rammer hit the wall. Its caterpillars slithered for a few seconds. Then they got a purchase and the wall went through, the rammer after it. Three Germans were trapped under the falling stones. The machine lurched up over the base of the wall and clawed its way over the fallen debris and the injured Germans. The air was full of alarmed cries.

Seconds later, Dipper Marsh sprang through the gap with his men. Working like demons they threw their grenades right and left. Men crumpled and fell before them. Marsh brought up his Bren and sprayed the Germans to the right. Another man did the same to the left. Lewis tore into the terraced vineyards. He threw out one clutch and brought the machine round, trailing the long fruit stalks with him.

Throwing the still caterpillar back into motion, he headed the machine back at the wall further up. A cry went up as Tufty led the rest of the company over the intervening ground.

Two of Marsh's men fell before a Spandau as another section of wall crashed down. Just as the volunteers were finding themselves in deadly peril through a ring of fire, Tufty leapt the second gap and hurled some grenades.

The Germans fell back down the terraces between the vines, firing as they retreated. Then the unexpected happened. An eight-inch projectile landed in the vineyard about thirty yards below the wall. More Germans were eliminated by it. Taking advantage of the sudden distraction, the commandos poured into them a hail of machine-gun and rifle fire.

As the grey-clad bodies piled up on the ground, the two forces slowly became numerically even. Lewis crashed back into the field as two more shells cratered the plantation only fifteen yards away.

'Get back through the wall!' Tufty yelled. 'We can fire over the top!'

For a few seconds, the wall which had played so vital a part in the engagement was a mass of scrambling men. Those who could not get through the gaps climbed over. Three commandos were winged with bullets.

A minute later, the positions had been completely reversed. It was the British who were thankful for the shelter of the wall and the Germans who were cursing it. Working methodically the commandos fired off useful bursts over the top of the wall. Every ten seconds, the naval shells crept closer to them. Few Germans escaped the horrifying chaos of the enclosed plantation. Some few who still hovered under the wall met with a quick death when grenades were dropped upon them.

As the German counter-fire ceased, Tufty ordered his men back into the wood. Lewis, having abandoned his machine during the shelling, came along with them. Six wounded men were being supported by their comrades, and five more had been left behind, dead.

These figures were the final casualty numbers for that engagement; excluding the bulldozer, which scattered sharp metal fragments in all directions after a direct hit.

18

That night, the commandos bivouacked in a derelict farmhouse. Shut in by the rain, they felt as if the whole world was theirs; that it was a small island scores of miles from anywhere. One thing they could do — unbidden — and that was sleep. Fit as they were, their whole bodies cried out for rest and recuperation.

After a luke-warm breakfast in a drizzly dawn, Captain Britwell had words to say to them. He looked round them in fatherly fashion. Since the beginning of the campaign in Italy they had become to him like his own family. A family for which his responsibility was great and unrelenting. A family which still shrank daily in spite of his best efforts.

He stood behind what had been the best table in the house, hands pressed on the top, face very serious.

'Men, in these last few hectic days, we've come to know each other well.

We've fought together and risked death together. I don't take our association lightly. If I survive, every one of your faces will be imprinted on my memory. Every time one of our comrades has been killed it has drawn us closer, depending upon each other the more for our confidence in what we still have to do.'

Scoop, standing at the back, stared round the sea of battered faces. He was greatly moved. These were the men who had won campaigns against odds. They would still do whatever was asked of them, even if it meant annihilation. They were inspired. And the man who was inspiring them, and had inspired them in the past, was his own brother, Jack.

Scoop was living one of his proudest moments.

It came at a time when his conscience had started to trouble him over the affair at the bridge. In seeking to assist Jack, and further the commandos' great record, he had violated his non-combatant status by taking up arms and killing at least one of the enemy.

The violation was a serious matter. If

any mention of what he had done leaked out to the Germans it could result in reprisals against his fellow war correspondents. The full knowledge of his misdemeanours had prompted him to make a momentous decision about his own future.

Jack was saying: 'At the present moment, we are a mile or two ahead of both the infantry and the armour. Ordinarily, the distance between would mean nothing, with no Germans to speak of between our forces and us, but with this rain, it means that we are cut off in time. We have the trucks and the fuel on which to run them. But if we go into Naples now — the first Allied troops to do so — we may be sharing that restless city with many times our own number of Germans.

'I cannot hazard a guess as to how long it will take the infantry spearhead, coming up the coast road past Pompeii, to reach the city. Neither can I tell how long the 7th Armoured Division will take on the inland route wide of our own. I have to make a last vital decision, and I want you to have a hand in it. Either we go on, we get the glory and take whatever hazards are in store for us, or we rest up until the Armoured Division finally catches up with us. Now, what do you say? Every man is free to speak.'

Tufty sank down on a three-legged rickety chair, a half smile playing round his rather thin mouth. He took out an almost empty packet of cigarettes and lit one.

For several seconds, only the sound of falling rain broke the silence, and then came the rumble of demolition from the harbour. The crashes of falling masonry filled the men with the old foreboding. The world was back with them, quite close.

A short, stocky individual with grey sideburns rose slowly to his feet. The others looked round at him. Lance-Corporal Tide was one of the oldest men in the detachment. He cleared his throat noisily.

'Well, Captain, I think I speak for all when I tell you us other ranks feel the same way about the mob as you do. Not many C.O.s would give us a chance to speak up like this. I for one am glad it's you who's still leading us. Moreover, I think you know we'll still do whatever you ask of us, regardless.'

The room was filled with a chorus of 'hear-hears' like a council meeting. Tufty nodded, looked down and blinked away an unheard of moisture from his eyes.

'Speaking for myself, I say go ahead, without waiting. Not for the glory — God forbid. But rather for the people of Naples who're waiting for us, and have been for some time. It was listening to them explosions just now made up my mind for me. Mostly it'll be harbour installations, but the Jerries are no respecters of persons, especially when they're having to pull out. These poor perishers have put up with years of Fascist domination. Then they've had the Jerries swarming all over them. Next it'll be us, but I've got a feeling they'll *want* us.'

Tide paused. He looked for a moment as though he was going to sit down, and then he thought better of it.

'As for the hazards, sir. Well, I'm not a deeply religious man, but I've got a feeling deep inside me which makes me think the 3rd Home Counties boys won't go under in Naples.'

He sat down suddenly and the room was full of a subdued murmur. Another man stood up unexpectedly. He was tall, lean and had close-set questing green eyes.

'You all know me, Shifty Rivers. I knew the Captain before most of you. I been inside a couple of times and when I tried to go straight it came a bit tough at first. A bunch o' tearaways started to smash up my caff one night. I was lucky, 'cause the Captain, there, happened to be passin' on his way to the theatre. He hopped straight in without hesitation, an' mopped up all three of them before you could say knife.

'I don't know why I'm tellin' you all this, except I feel the Captain ought to have a medal. Now, if he was to be the first officer into Naples, the perishin' High Command couldn't hum an' hah about it. I vote we go on!'

Rivers sat down, and Dipper Marsh said his piece. They put the matter to the vote and all forty-odd of them wanted to go forward without delay. Britwell thanked them with an unaccustomed show of emotion. Half an hour later, they were slowly moving into the city in convoy.

The canvas covers of the trucks had been removed for observation purposes, in spite of the rain. The men sat erect, weapons cradled against any emergency. Occasionally they were sniped at, but there was no serious opposition to stop them.

Soon, they were in the outskirts of the ruined city. Each man, full of his own private thoughts, stared humbly at the dismal spectacle of shattered houses, many of which bore testimony to the destructive power of Allied bombers.

Although they did not know it at the time, they were to learn later that the town was without water. The great city aqueduct had been cut in seven places by the indifferent Germans. The power station had been destroyed. All spare food had been removed. Countless buildings had been rigged with bombs and booby traps, to go off at some time in the future — a menace to soldier and civilian alike.

The outskirts were not as deserted as they seemed.

In a matter of minutes, the vehicles were surrounded by swarming crowds of Neapolitans, old and young, male and female. Girls and women fought to get near the commandos, half pulling them out of their trucks in order to plant a kiss on their lips. Fruit, nuts and other luxuries appeared as if by magic. Some of it was handed over, and much more was dropped from the upper windows of the shattered houses.

Their ears rang to the endlessly chanted cry of 'Viva, viva!' Soon, the trucks were covered in fruit and nuts. The level mounted until it was up round the thighs of the grinning soldiers.

This adulation went on for a mile or so, until debris and fallen masonry made it imperative to leave the vehicles. They were directed to leave them in an open courtyard, where a whole squad of youthful boys and girls promised to mount guard over them with their lives.

Reduced to weapons again, and what they could easily carry, the commandos gradually left the excited population behind. Nearer the docks, the Germans were still known to be in some force.

A last battle had to be fought.

★   ★   ★

The entry to the harbour was a typical commando job of work. Strung out under cover at points ranging from fifty to a hundred yards, they studied the layout. The wall was ten feet high, but in three places the top of it had crumbled under bomb or shellfire. To the left of the open space on which they were deployed, there was a wide gate in an arch.

Grenades were lobbed into it, and ten men, half of them with machine-guns, walked steadily towards it, firing bursts as they went. Three of them crumbled as their fire was returned, but the rest kept on.

Three other teams of ten raced forward towards the crumpled sections of the wall. As they went, they extended between them long collapsible commando-type ladders. These they hooked over the top and proceeded to climb. Only one team had any serious difficulty. More grenades eased their progress. In five minutes, the gate had been forced and thirty-five men, led by Britwell and Marsh, were assembled near the gate, rapidly assimilating their next move.

Dusty Lewis, who had stayed with the party after the loss of his last bulldozer, stood on the bomb-shattered open space until all had vanished. He had been offered the chance of going over the wall with the climbers, but he had declined, thinking that the ladders might be placed under too much strain by his weight.

When all the rest had gone, he walked across with Scoop and entered the gateway unmolested. Sounds of demolition still came from the wharves. Most of it came from the north side.

'We're aiming to get control of the southern wharves,' Tufty explained, as the last two figures approached his group. Taking what cover they could, the commandos moved off in small groups, filtering through idle railway wagons, and scouting the offices and storerooms as they went. As they progressed, it became evident that a steady fire was keeping out the small ships wide of the harbour. It came from the north side, where the demolitions were taking place.

Sad sights met their eyes from time to time.

Many small ships had been sunk at their moorings. Their masts and salt-caked smoke stacks looked pathetic, slanting out of the water in all directions. A floating dock had capsized with a small steamer in it.

Slowly and methodically, the commandos fought their way from building to building, steadily gaining ground. Soon, they were on the southern wharf. In a roofless single-storey office block, they studied the situation afresh.

Scoop Britwell and Dusty Lewis moved in behind them. Almost at once, the big man started to show a marked interest in the two-hundred-and-fifty ton crane, which towered up from the wharf side some sixty yards away. On the top of it was a movable arm, and mobile on the arm's upper rails was a glassed control cabin.

'Just look at that mob!' Lewis shouted hoarsely.

Scoop followed the direction of his pointing finger through the window space. Four Germans were running for the foot of the crane, obviously bent on its destruction. 88mm. shells were firing across the dockyard now, but Lewis characteristically ignored them. Instead, he looked round for weapons. He grabbed a handful of grenades, tucked them into his shirt, and picked up a Bren gun as though it were a toy.

Out he went, through the back of the building. Seconds later, Scoop saw him haring along the wharf in pursuit of the would-be-wreckers. One man already had his feet on the winding ladder up the vertical part of the crane. The others had reached the foot. Pausing in his run, Lewis hurled one grenade and then another. A German aimed a machine-pistol at him, but his sighting was inaccurate. He was eliminated with the other two when the grenades exploded viciously almost on top of them. One moment the men were standing on the alert and the next, amid a billowing grey cloud, edged with orange flame, they were no more.

Lewis ran on through the smoke. He mounted the metal ladder without hesitation. Two turns above him, the remaining German peered back at him, breathless and tense of face. He ran on, scarcely pausing. From the north side, a long stream of bright tracer reached out after Lewis, but he was moving very quickly.

As the fugitive made the last turn above him, Lewis fired a burst from his Bren. Wounded, the soldier clawed himself erect and disappeared from view. He had reached the arm. Lewis raced on, breathing with difficulty through his mouth. The breeze would have rocked a less stoutly built man moving at that speed, two steps at a time.

Suddenly, a grenade rolled down the steps to meet him. He saw it, made an animal noise in his throat, and dropped back a few steps, turning an angle and throwing himself flat. Fortunately for him, the grenade exploded while still well above him. Two steel steps and a part of the rail had disappeared, but the pioneer made light of the obstacle.

He began to move more quietly, with

the Bren angled, barrel upwards, across his body. One cautious step at a time, he waited for the German to show himself. He was not disappointed. A quick burst from the Bren and a cry carried to him which could only mean that the man was hit again.

Throwing caution to the winds, Lewis raced up the remaining steps. The German was prostrate on the platform, making an effort to raise his weapon. Lewis threw the Bren at him, like a club. The butt caught the German in the neck. He lost consciousness as the gun clattered down beside him.

Lewis was ruthless with him. He rolled the unconscious body off the platform. It sailed down, arms and legs awry, until it hit the wharf with a dull thud. Scoop, who had watched the whole of Lewis's manoeuvre, felt a sickening in the stomach.

Through his glasses, the journalist watched with mounting curiosity. Two minutes later, Lewis's body, dwarfed by the height, took its place in the mobile cabin. He must have had no difficulty with the controls, because the cabin started to roll forward on the mobile arm.

To think that the fellow might still be carrying packages on some southern beach, Scoop thought, as he watched. Whereas, technically speaking, he's really a deserter.

The cabin came to a smooth halt at the end of the arm. Ignoring the hail of bullets flying across to their hideout, Scoop watched breathlessly for developments. As usual, Lewis did not take long to get into action.

From the window of his eyrie, he weighed up the situation beneath and beyond him. He spat upon his hands. Clearly, on the other side of the dock, he could see the 88mm. gunners working hard behind their shields. He, himself, appeared to have been forgotten for the time being.

He studied the wind, weighing two grenades carefully in a giant hand. Although he knew nothing of the acceleration of a falling body, he felt sure his four-second grenades would reach their targets before exploding. He studied the distance and the angle, with all the care of a would-be prize-winner in a fairground.

'I wish you were 'ere to see this, Nip,' he muttered.

Pulling out a pin, he launched his first missile. It fell and exploded ten feet in front of the nearest 88mm. gun. One of the team crumpled, but the others survived.

His second shot was a 'bull'. It landed right on the gun, scattering weapon and crew. A hoarse cheer went up from his side of the harbour. A spurt of tracer fell woefully short beneath him. His fourth grenade knocked off the barrel of a second gun and shattered the crew. Survivors raced for the protection of the buildings behind them.

He sent a burst of Bren fire after them.

The encounter was reduced to small arms fire from that moment. The lull was timely. Tufty Britwell rose to his feet and moved round his men.

'Conserve your ammunition, lads,' he warned them. 'Stocks are getting low. There's no knowing how long we shall have to hang on here.'

19

The afternoon dragged. Firing on the German side of the harbour had been cut to a minimum. No attempt was made to retake the southern side of the harbour, but the commandos were uncomfortably aware that their opponents had not retired. It could only mean one thing. They had been ordered to harass any attempt at getting into the harbour from the sea.

Lewis, up on his crane, had the best view of the sea. He had studied the concourse of ships for over half an hour before weariness made him fall asleep in his padded seat in the cabin.

About five p.m. he was roused by the start of a naval shoot against the north side of the harbour. About half a dozen ships took part in it, firing — so far as he could estimate — six-inch and four-inch guns. It was an experience which would have shaken lesser men to see the dark shadows erupt from the smoking, flame-fringed gun barrels to arc through the sky perilously close to his perch.

As it was, he passed the time chewing walnuts and heaving their shells in handfuls into the placid waters beneath him. Wall after wall of the buildings opposite crumbled and slid down into untidy heaps of masonry. He could not have done a better job of demolition himself without an outsize 'dozer.

'Somethink's goin' to 'appen,' he kept muttering to himself with his mouthful.

Twenty minutes later, something did. A single landing craft started to move forward from the anchorage, under the hail of shells. His first thought was that it must be L.C.T. 17. But then he reflected that there were dozens of them, all alike in design. And it was too far away to see the markings.

A single, probing hostile gun, started to feel the range of the harbour from several miles to the north-east. It served as a reminder that there was much fighting still to be done before the port could be said to be in Allied hands. Once a minute, it pumped heavy projectiles into the harbour waters.

Lewis wondered at its inaccuracy. He squinted out to sea again. The L.C.T. was moving in steadily at eight or nine knots. Further out, men were pouring from the L.S.T.s into the tiny assault craft, hanging from their falls. The navy was having a go at last. A sweet bit of action could not be many minutes away. He rubbed his hands in gleeful anticipation. Maybe he could put the great crane to some real use shortly . . .

★　★　★

L.C.T. 17, with all hands on the alert for any kind of emergency, was making her bid to clear the harbour entrance. Rawson had been warned that the obstruction was heavy and that his ship might not have the power to move it. Nevertheless, his scheme had received official blessing, and he had decided to go through with it.

A furlong offshore, he clamped the glasses to his tired eyes and searched the area of the entrance for sign of the obstruction. At that distance, it remained hidden. Latest information had said that British units were believed to have control of the south side of the harbour.

He panned his glasses round. Even at that distance, the tips of the masts of sunken ships could be identified with ease. Only the big crane looked usable. He wondered if there was anyone capable of operating it. His jaw tightened spasmodically as the projectiles continued to sail through the air over his head. This was a sea-land job. There were no aircraft about. Not that they mightn't take a hand later.

Tracers started to clang against his bow door, by way of welcome. The northern wharves certainly were hostile. He hoped that nothing untoward would happen in the entrance. The worst that could happen would be for his ship to be sunk on top of the wreck already there. That would take some sorting out!

A hundred yards away, he cut the speed to half ahead. There was no point in charging headlong into something one could not see. Signalman Joyce was in the bows, his low brow almost invisible under a big steel helmet which he wore over his right ear. He was studying the entrance through a spare pair of glasses. Suddenly he spotted the blunt bows, underside towards him.

'Obstruction in sight, sir!' he called excitedly.

Rawson left his bridge and raced forward down the port side. It took him but a few seconds to size up the job and then he ran back again, shouting: 'All hands, stand by!'

He called down to Jock Dodd to inform him the job was about to commence, and had Jones alter course five points to starboard. Squarely behind his binnacle, he awaited the impact with nerves under rigid control.

The seconds dragged. Then came the scraping impact when everybody clutched for hand holds. The bows rose a couple of feet before slipping back again with an unsettling grinding noise. Rawson rang for Full Ahead Both. Again the clang on metal. The wreck shifted a few inches. The crew groaned as the bows scraped again and slid sharply out of the water.

Rawson killed the speed and went astern.

'I'm going to try another run, Swain. This time I'm going to hit it at speed, and from a slightly different angle. Got any bright ideas?'

Jones glanced up to the bridge. 'Not really, sir, unless you think having all hands forrard would help!'

'We'll try it!'

Rawson called the engine-room again, and informed all on deck through his hailer. Ten men, including the stokers and cook, ran forward and assembled in the fore part of the well-deck, just behind the bow doors.

'This is the nearest we'll ever get to going ashore through them doors,' Joyce remarked without humour.

"Ow you can talk like that when we might get pitched through 'em in a couple of minutes, I don't know,' a stoker grumbled, still breathless from his run up from below. He felt out of place doing any sort of duty in the open air.

Another stream of tracer clanged

against the door.

'Who's that knocking at my door?' another wag queried in a piping treble voice.

Others glowered at him, but their brows went up when he started to inflate his lifebelt. Those who were wearing theirs followed suit. The ship's revs built up quickly. Quick moves on the part of the skipper and cox'n brought her round in a fine arc to starboard and then back on course. The screws raced. The wake frothed and piled up as high as it ever could with a maximum speed of nine knots.

Joyce was singing: '*Why are we waiting?*' rather untunefully when the second sickening crash occurred. All the ten men were hurled into the ramp as it reverberated and leapt a few inches to meet them.

Rawson was reciting all the naval oaths he had ever heard as the plates shook beneath him and the bows started to rear up again. An ear-shattering sound caused by rending metal tortured the waiting crew as they awaited the outcome.

'It's going to be all right, sir!' Jones yelled.

He had noticed the slow forward motion of the vessel. The wreck was indeed giving way before the L.C.'s stubborn onslaught. The bows rode still higher, and the bridge and superstructure canted backwards. Down below, Petty Officer Dodd was shouting unheard.

The stunned men in the well-deck slowly recovered to find a sizeable jet of water pouring in on them. A leak had been sprung in the door. The ship shook as though it were piling up on rocks. And then the obstruction slid away from her bows into deeper water. The barge had rolled over, on its side. The L.C. bounced twice before its bows dropped again, and then it charged forward.

Something scraped along the flat bottom and passed between the screws aft.

'Starboard your helm, Swain, we've made it!' Rawson yelled, his oaths forgotten.

He cut the speed again, and headed into the harbour, breathing hard as though he had just finished a marathon run.

'We're leaking forrard, sir!' Joyce called, running aft.

Rawson followed the rating's pointing finger. His face twisted up in anguish. So great had been his relief when the wreck gave before them, that he had not noticed the damage. Already a foot of water was swishing about in the well.

'We'll have to run her in quickly, Swain!'

The crew could tell by his tone that he knew the ship was doomed. They did not need to be told that *abandon ship* was near. Those who had scorned lifebelts rushed to the messdeck to find them. They emerged again, hurriedly puffing air into them.

The ship had increased speed and turned for the southern wharf. Rawson could see anxious faces in the buildings no doubt weighing up their chances of reaching the side.

'Stand by the rails!' he shouted. 'If you have to swim it won't be for long.'

Close range weapons opened up on

them again, crowding the men to starboard. From the southern wharf came a brief retaliatory fire.

'At least we've got friends ashore,' Jones muttered.

With fifty yards to go, he lashed the wheel and joined the others, also blowing up his belt. Suddenly a movement caught his eye. The giant crane arm above them was moving. He pointed, and Rawson saw it, too. He stood amazed, clutching the starboard bridge rail, mouth agape. A giant hook was dangling some twenty feet above and behind them. Slowly, the great arm followed them. The hook came nearer. Jock Dodd panted up behind him, breathless and startled at what he saw for the first time.

The well deck was nearly half full. The ship was quickly losing way, although her engines were still doing maximum revolutions.

'You might have reminded me to bring a lifebelt,' Dodd grumbled hoarsely.

'You may not need it yet,' Rawson told him, still watching the hook.

Suddenly the hook dropped lower and

clattered against the stern rail. 'Help me make it fast!' called Rawson.

Jones, Dodd and two other men joined him, and together they hauled in the hook. It was a struggle, but they managed to make a turn round the capstan and fasten the hook onto the rope.

'For God's sake tighten her,' Jones muttered, staring at the hook.

He glanced round at the wharf, still some thirty-five yards away. A small group of soldiers had appeared and were watching anxiously, but there was nothing they could do, except wait to fish them out of the drink.

'The driver's spotted us,' Rawson croaked. 'He's hauling her in! Stand back!'

Standing back was harder to do than anyone would think. At that moment, the decks were steeply canted forward, making it difficult to maintain any balance. The crane hook and hawser took the strain, and the ship lost way altogether. The capstan creaked, but it held.

'Get right aft!' Rawson yelled.

The bows disappeared in a sudden rush, leaving the stern suspended on the hook. Two of the hands went over the side to appear spluttering and shouting in a few seconds. The others clung to the bridge, the quarterdeck rail and the hatch covers. The stern swung shorewards, with all eyes turned aloft, watching the arm which bore the weight.

Two minutes later, the wrecked vessel clanged against the more substantial wharf wall. The stern was just about on a level with the top. Eager hands stretched out to pull them ashore. Three men were clear when the capstan gave a queer metallic groan. It appeared to be straining away from the deck plates.

'Hurry it up, lads, she's going!'

One after another the crew jumped for the wharf. Some only just managed to grip the edge and had to be hauled in. Rawson went last. His wet seaboots slithered from under him and he dropped on his face, peering backwards.

He was in time to see the capstan wrenched out of the deck like a drawn tooth. The L.C. fell away with a mighty splash which threw harbour water all over them. Spluttering unhappily, they had to dodge the flying capstan on the lashing hook. There were no casualties. They had only their own safety to think about.

'Better make a quick run for cover, lads,' Dipper Marsh warned.

The L.C.'s crew scrambled after him. They were still under the effects of an unpleasant shock, and now here was a pleasant one which they were slow to comprehend.

Tracer arced over them as they ran for the back of the buildings. Willing hands drew them inside the open door. Soon the building was full. Rawson was the last man in. He gaped round the assembled soldiers. Finally his blinking eyes settled on Tufty Britwell. Scoop moved alongside his brother.

'Saints alive,' Rawson muttered, scratching his bald patch. He had lost his cap in the last desperate scramble. 'Britwell and Britwell! I don't believe it!'

The tension went out of the commandos. The room filled with good humour and light-hearted chaffing.

'You won't believe who the bloke is on top of that crane, either, I suppose,' Tufty said, slapping him on the back.

Rawson crossed to the window. He peered up at the crane, striving to identify its driver. 'No, it couldn't be,' he decided. 'Whoever it is, we owe a lot to him, I suppose. When do we get a chance to talk to him?'

'Not for a while yet, anyway,' Scoop interposed. 'It's started to rain again!'

20

Many eyes had seen with great satisfaction the last telling action of L.C.T. 17. As she steamed through the harbour entrance the fleet standing by came alive with flags fluttering at the halyards and Aldis lamp messages winking interminably from the bridges.

In quick succession, over a score of small fast L.C.A.s — Landing Craft Assault — were lowered into the water and started for shore. Each craft, although possessing a crew of only four, carried about forty fully-armed naval commandos.

These men had been in a state of readiness for over twenty-four hours. It felt good to be on the way. In good order, the craft converged on the harbour entrance, taking their places in line. Another naval bombardment heralded their approach. Shell after shell whistled over them from cruisers, destroyers and flak ships.

Only when the first three assault boats were well up harbour and heading for the northern wharf did the shoot fade out. One after the other they reached for and tied up to the stone steps.

A heartening fire from the south side held the German defenders in check, as the the first naval men scrambled up the steps. Dusty Lewis, still up aloft, saw it all from a bird's eye view. Tufty and company were throwing into the crucial assault the last of their valuable ammunition. The naval boys could not know that they were nearly out, but at this stage it was too late to matter.

Half the first boat load became casualties, in spite of Britwell's crossfire, but after that the British gradually got on top. Ten assault boats pulled in at the northern steps altogether. Almost four hundred men joined in winkling out the stubborn rearguard defenders. Their task was rendered easier because the Germans were also running out of ammunition. Two more craft came ashore where Britwell's party were holed up. They handed over their spare ammunition before moving off as part of the plan to ring the harbour.

The rest of the L.C.A.s moved straight up harbour, dodging the sunken wrecks until they grounded on a launching runway. The distant gun had ceased to drop projectiles in the harbour some forty minutes earlier. There were no signs of the expected German reinforcements.

Everything fell a little on the flat side for those men who had been there longest. Britwell's men and Rawson's crew grew tired of swopping yarns and many of them started to doze fitfully. Only Dusty could see anything to stay awake for.

Close on the heels of the assault boats, L.C.T.s and lighters were moving in, piled high with crates, ammunition boxes and all the accoutrements of war. His eyes gleamed as he thought what might be among them.

One of the foremost ships flashed a message to him. He had no idea of morse, but he went through the motions of lining up his crane to begin the unloading. This was what the ship's crews had intended. Overalled sailors swarmed ashore, and peaked-capped petty officers waved signs to him as successive nets of stores were slung on his hook.

Time passed quickly. He was far from bored. Only the void in his stomach told him all was not well with him. He was hungry. Towards dusk, a group of pioneers came ashore to start moving away the stores. He was not to know for some time that they were his mates from way back. But they found out he was up aloft by making contact with the sailors in the building.

When they waved, he waved back automatically. He worked like an automaton, hoisting, swinging round and lowering; back over the ships again, and start the operation over again. From time to time, he yawned hugely. But still he watched the stores as he landed them. Lamps were rigged, so that the unloading could continue. About nine o'clock he unloaded four bulldozers, one after the other; all fully erected and ready for work. He began to feel like a change, but still the ships swung into the wharf and their crews expected him to carry on.

Down in the building, Scoop Britwell was finishing off a meal which had been hastily put together from tins brought ashore.

He said to Lofty Rawson: 'You know that chap, Dusty, is the most amazing fellow I've ever met. Left alone with a job to do, he's worth half a regiment!'

Rawson nodded tiredly. The loss of his craft was still bothering him. 'He's a pocket Hercules, and no mistake. There was a time when I thought sacrificing my ship just wasn't worth while, but finding you chaps ashore, waiting for us, put a different complexion on things. I've been privileged to see what a wonderful job these commandos have done. Trouble is, most of what they've done will go unmentioned and unsung.'

'Unless I can do something about it,' Scoop remarked, quietly.

Rawson looked into Britwell's eyes, seeing him as though for the first time. His voice trembled with emotion when he said: 'Give 'em a good write-up, lad.'

'I will,' Scoop promised. 'And your boys, too!'

Rawson turned away abruptly and fumbled with a cigarette.

★　★　★

Half an hour later, Scoop started the ascent of the crane. He was loaded down with an armful of articles. Carefully wrapped to keep them warm, he had a huge plateful of bacon, beans, and sausages. Stuffed in his pockets were two cans of export beer, and an unopened tin of pears.

He also had with him a signal pad, binoculars, two pencils, a torch, a tin of fifty cigarettes and a box of matches. He fought his way along the high metal gangway against a biting wind and driving rain. When he reached the mobile cabin he was almost done in. Dusty eased him into the spare seat, and sniffed appreciatively.

Scoop uncovered the food and felt a great pleasure as the big man's eyes blinked over it.

'Supper time at last,' Dusty breathed.

He set up his levers in neutral and

handled the plate with great care. After about five minutes, an angry voice called up from below on a loud-hailer. Scoop's face clouded with anger.

He stepped out into the air. 'What do you mean 'what's going on up there?' The crane-driver's stopped for a snack, that's what! Now clear off and let him eat!'

'We can't stop now,' the anxious naval lieutenant bellowed, 'there's five more ships waiting for unloading.'

'Then they'll just have to wait, won't they!' Scoop shouted.

He dropped an empty beer can in the direction of the voice and retired inside the cabin. The officer called again two or three times in the next fifteen minutes, but his calls were in vain.

Dusty was slowly working his way through the tinned fruit, and Scoop was scribbling thoughtfully on his pad. When he was good and finished, and a sweet Virginia cigarette was going in his mouth, Lewis threw open the door. He took a few gulps of fresh air, leaned over the side and launched his empties at the wharf.

Finally, he went back to work. Scoop

scribbled on, glancing from time to time at Lewis's sweating frame. Inspiration came easily. He hoped his final report on the campaign up to Naples would go through verbatim.

About ten o'clock, most of the human flies down below were pointing and gesticulating towards the town. Scoop focused his glasses and was able to see easily, thanks to a full moon. His pulses quickened with pride at what he saw.

'Hey, Scoop, what's that 'orrible row I keep 'earing?' Dusty asked, without looking round.

'It's the sound of bagpipes, Dusty. The infantry have arrived in force up the coast road. I can see them clearly, marching four abreast. It's a great sight!'

Dusty had a look for himself. Scoop could tell he was impressed, but all he said was: 'Fancy bringin' bloomin' bagpipes on a perishin' jaunt like this!'

Scoop chuckled. The people of Naples were giving the troops a great welcome, although the power and the water were cut off.

'What you goin' to do now the

fighting's finished round 'ere?' Dusty wanted to know.

Scoop put down his glasses and took time to think that one over. He said: 'Well, I've got to get this last despatch away first. It's the end of a series called 'Naples or Die'. Then, after that I'm taking a bit of time off. In any case, this will probably be the last despatch I shall write this war. Do you remember the farm where we met that day — where the woman called Violetta made us food?'

Dusty nodded.

'Well, just before that I met a girl. An Italian called Marisa. I said I'd go back and see her after Naples. And I reckon I'm due for a break, don't you?'

'When will you be pullin' out?'

'It won't be before tomorrow evening, I should think. The army censors take ages to get the stuff away.'

Dusty rubbed his hands. He said: 'That'll suit me fine. Tomorrow morning I'll get in a few hours exercise on one o' them new bulldozers, an' then I'll be ready to come with you. I've got a hankerin' to take another look at that

Violetta. So long as my Lucy don't find out!'

Scoop laughed out loud. 'I'll be glad of your company, but don't you think you might have trouble getting away?'

Dusty gave a deep belly laugh.

'You ain't serious, are you, cocker? Me 'ave trouble in gettin' away? That's a laugh an' no mistake! Why, if they tried to stop me, I'd drive one o' them bulldozers straight through the Military Police barracks!'

Scoop said: 'I believe you would, too.' But he was thinking that a few chosen words in the right quarters by his brother, Rawson and himself, would render such measures unnecessary.

Presently, Dusty gave him an odd look.

'What did you mean when you said this will be the last despatch you'll write this war?'

'After this visit to Marisa I'm taking down my war correspondent's flashes for good. I'm finished as a non-combatant. My next problem is to make up my mind which fighting unit to join. What do you suggest?'

The ex-boxer's slitted eyes opened as far as they would go. 'You're stoppin' bein' a non-combatant? You mean you're finishin' sendin' despatches back to the *Globe*? What in the world put that idea into your head?'

Scoop explained how he had used a grenade and a Bren gun at the bridge crossing while Dusty was away having his bulldozer repaired. Dusty shook his head.

'I suppose it was wrong of you, but who's to know? Your brother's men won't blab an' neither will I. You ought to stay as you are. You like freedom same as I do. Mebbe we could move on to Rome together. Me mother always wanted to see Rome.'

'It's no good, chum, my mind's made up,' Scoop insisted. 'I've killed at least one German. It's a matter of conscience. Now, have you got any useful suggestions, or not?'

A short spell of concentrated thinking contorted Dusty's face. 'It's 'ard to advise you. In a way, you've been a commando already. You've been with the infantry and sailed with the navy. No, mate, I don't reckon I can 'elp you. Why don't you 'old on for a bit, an' ask the Italian girl friend?'

Scoop nodded. The more he thought about it the more he felt certain that Marisa was the one to ask.

He said: 'Okay, Dusty, I'll do that. Ask Marisa, I mean. Maybe we can have a little party or two while we're there!'

The big man beamed. 'I'm with you on that, mate. Rome's been built a long time. I reckon it can wait a day or two for us. What do you say?'

THE END

We do hope that you have enjoyed reading this large print book.

Did you know that all of our titles are available for purchase?

We publish a wide range of high quality large print books including:
Romances, Mysteries, Classics
General Fiction
Non Fiction and Westerns

Special interest titles available in large print are:
The Little Oxford Dictionary
Music Book, Song Book
Hymn Book, Service Book

Also available from us courtesy of Oxford University Press:
Young Readers' Dictionary
(large print edition)
Young Readers' Thesaurus
(large print edition)

For further information or a free brochure, please contact us at:
Ulverscroft Large Print Books Ltd.,
The Green, Bradgate Road, Anstey,
Leicester, LE7 7FU, England.
Tel: (00 44) **0116 236 4325**
Fax: (00 44) **0116 234 0205**

Other titles in the
Linford Mystery Library:

JOURNEY INTO TERROR

E. C. Tubb

The first exploratory expedition to
Pluto returns with the Captain, Jules
Carmodine, alone . . . What happened
to the crew remains a mystery as
Carmodine is suffering from amnesia,
and mentally and physically broken in
health. Later, although his health
improves, the amnesia remains. Then,
when Carmodine is forced to return
to Pluto, he faces a journey into terror.
He must remember what happened on
that first mission — otherwise the second
expedition will suffer exactly the same
fate as the first . . .

SWARTHYFACE

Norman Lazenby

Kennedy Balfour, ex-RAF in post-war Britain, helps a frightened young woman on a train, but doesn't realise what he's getting into. He only knows that Delia Thomas is beautiful, and terrified of the man following her. Apparently the man, known as 'Swarthyface', is a criminal mastermind and his main target is the girl's father. And if Balfour persists in protecting the girl and her father, then one of them would die . . . and that someone might very well be himself . . .

THE SLITHERERS

John Russell Fearn

The obscure village of Coxwold had suddenly become the centre of attention of every daily newspaper. People from all over had descended upon it, investigating, questioning, and sending reports to London. Something had happened in a nearby wheat field which had reduced two normal, healthy men to insanity and death. The police, suspecting foul play, lacked any evidence. So what could it be that had driven the victims to madness? This was unlike any crime ever before recorded . . .

ESCAPE INTO SPACE

E. C. Tubb

Geldray, working for the government in building a starship, fears world destruction. So he privately plans to make the vessel a colonising project. Meanwhile, power-crazed Edward Smith intends to destroy all obstacles in his way — including Geldray, project Star and the politician Melgrath's reputation — in order to take over the government. Realising Smith's intentions, Geldray's last act is to launch the starship. Will the ship's crew succeed in escaping into space to find a new home amongst the stars?

THE GOLDEN GNOME

Leslie Wilkie

A land ownership dispute and the finding of a hidden safe lead to Jennifer Beddows employing a private detective, Terry Jagger, to help investigate her grandfather's background. Together the pair uncover the secret of what lay beneath the waters of a mysterious tropical atoll and of the murders that led to its discovery.